MW01532377

To My Mom
She is smart and courageous and compassionate and stong and
amazing and badass. If I am able to be any of those things it is
because of her. I don't get there without her having been there
first.
Much love and light.

We only ever know other people through the lenses of our own perceptions. These perceptions are shaped by our every experience and belief, and they are as unique as our fingerprints. Our perceptions may shift as we grow older and obtain wisdom and experience but they remain ours alone. No other person will ever be able to see the world exactly as we see it, through our lens.

Because of our unique perspective, we will never completely know other people. This is even true for the people we love best in the world. This is perhaps especially true for the people we love best in the world. Not only do we see the things we want to sometimes, we see the things we are *able* to see.

We are all amazingly complex. We are a mix of "good" and "bad". Light and dark. We are never all one or the other. In fact, life is balance and one does not exist without the other. Yin and Yang. It makes us interesting. It makes relationships complicated. It is both the curse and the gift of our humanity.

And you shall sorrow
For to love is to lose
It is the inevitability of proximity
Your participation is optional
But your choices are limited.
And you shall sorrow
The game is rigged
You might win through sheer dumb luck
But not always through your efforts
And never as much as you might like
And you shall sorrow
If only heartbreak
Immunized you against having your heart
broken again
But it doesn't work that way
You shall sorrow.
T.F. Forester

July
Obituary

Allison (Grant) Montebello (41)

Allison (Grant) Montebello died unexpectedly on Tuesday July 1, 2014 after an auto accident. Allison leaves her husband of 20 years, David Montebello, three daughters, Jenna (19), April (15) and Charlotte (12) her mother, Cynthia Grant and many, many friends. Allison was a devoted wife and mother who volunteered for the Greenwald PTA. Allison loved to read and was an excellent photographer who won a Miller Fellowship for photography in 2012. She was also worked part time as a marketing consultant.

From the police blotter

At approximately 2:45am on July 1st, police responded to a single car accident at Evergreen Pond on Post Road. A 2008 Ford Explorer was found partially submerged in the pond. A single occupant was pulled from the vehicle but was unresponsive. Police preformed CPR at the scene but the driver was later declared dead at Bethany Hospital. The victim was identified as Allison Montebello of Greenwald. Alcohol and speed may have been factors in the crash. Police are investigating.

"They will buy tickets to your triumphs
They love you for your successes
But the seats beyond the footlights
Remain empty
For your disasters
Your dismay and heartbrokenness
Belong to you alone."
T.F. Forester

Allison's Journal Entry dated August 15, 2012
Almost two years before the accident

I've applied for a photography fellowship. I'm not sure that my photographs are good enough for such a thing. I don't know that any of me is good enough. I'm not sure what I was thinking by applying. I get impulsive sometimes and do crazy stuff. Sometimes my intuition is very good and I trust it. Other times. Like now, I can't seem to access it. David and Sarah and my mom all say that I'm awesome and I shouldn't worry. But I don't feel awesome. And I worry. All. Of. The. Time. I try not to let the girls see it though. I want them to be strong, amazing women. I never want them to feel fear like I do.

I got my first camera on my ninth birthday. It was a gift from my father, in the middle of one of the longest periods of time, when he was actually around. My mother was furious about that camera. I blew out the candles on my cake and she handed me a nice little pile of gifts; a poster of a band I liked at the time a book I'd been hoping to read and nice pair gold wishbone earrings. Mom had let me get my ears pierced a few weeks before and this would be the first pair of earrrings I could wear when I took the starters out. The carefully printed tag said that the gifts were from Mom and Dad although I knew, even at nine, that Mom had picked them out and likely paid for them as well. His name was attached as a courtesy. Or a dig.

After I opened them Dad suddenly exclaimed, "We forgot one!"

"We forgot one what?" my mother asked him with annoyance. She was clearly not privy to whatever this surprise was and her irritation at this last minute inclusion was clear.

"One of Allie's gifts," my father said like this was the most natural thing in the world.

He was the only one who ever called me Allie. I really liked it. My mother loathed it. I was never sure if he did it to please me or aggravate her. Maybe it was both.

"Well, let's give it to her then," she said tersely.

She was still trying to preserve the facade of unity. We all knew better. My father wasn't having it.

"I got you this," he said beaming and pulling a brown paper bag from under the kitchen table.

My mother worked hard to maintain control. My father was spontaneous, unpredictible and often unreliable. I was good at reading other people's emotions, even then and I knew that Mom was livid at what she perceived as an ambush. I was too excited to find out what was in the bag to care.

It was a really nice camera. It had multiple lenses and looked incredibly complicated. I must have looked a little overwhelmed because he said, "I'll show you how it works, Allie."

My mother said, "We'll be right back, honey. You can keep looking at it." She gave my father a look which brooked no defiance and cocked her head toward the other room, indicating that he's best follow her. He smiled at me and he went.

I could hear the beginning of the argument and then pieces of it later after my mother admonished my father to "keep his voice down for God's sake". I was used to their arguing. I tuned a lot of it out. My mother said things about it being too expensive and made a snide remark about the camera "falling off a truck." I didn't know what that meant at nine. That statement made me panic briefly and check my gift for damage but none seemed apparent. My mother clearly didn't want me to have this gift. I'd only had it for five minutes but already I was enamored beyond anything and I knew I would fight her for the right to keep it.

It never came to that though. Somehow, she capituplated. My father, true to his word, did show me how to use it. I picked up the basics fast. My father marveled that I had an inate talent. I think it was more because I was a devoted student. I wanted to learn eveything I could.

My father had been in and out of my life for years at that point. A few months after the commencement of the photography lessons, he disappeared again. When he returned, my mother presented him with her ultimatum and that was the end of that.

I know that above all, my mother wanted stability for my life. I get it. Stability is important. As I get older though, I think that maybe it isn't all black and white. Sometimes people are doing the best that they can. Their best may not be what you were hoping for but maybe you should still let them try.

My mother has no idea, but I looked him up. Later, when the internet became a thing and then later again on Facebook, I looked him up. He lives in Rhode Island. He is married with a kid who is significantly younger than me. It looks like a perfectly average life. Maybe he changed. Maybe he just couldn't make domesticity work woth us. I have never contacted him but every so often, I stalk his page.

I wonder if it's too late to take back my application for the fellowship. The guy I met at the gallery was super nice and he seemed to think I had a good shot at winning. But maybe I should tell him it's all been big mistake. It was a misunderstanding. In a weak moment, I pretended I have more talent than I really have. I'm not actually any good at this. I'm not sure I'm actually any good at anything. It probably doesn't matter. I'm not going to win a thing like that anyway.

*"Tell me all of your beautiful, luminous
secrets
Lay bare your truth, he said
I have but one precious, glimmering secret
She whispered
And it is you."*
T.F. Forester

Adam
July
Five Days After the Accident

I didn't want to go to Allison's funeral. I didn't want to see her daughters and her husband. I didn't want to be infected by their sadness. That sounds callous, I know. It wasn't as if I had no sadness of my own. I had plenty. But their sadness was innocent. Mine was tainted by guilt. I had said goodbye to her that night and I wanted no part of goodbyes at the funeral home. I had to go though. After all, I am Adam Miller. I'm the guy who used his trust fund and his talent to create a photography fellowship and Allison won that fellowship.

I would have gone to the funeral of any of my other students. Although, I wasn't sleeping with any of my other students. Did that make it better or worse? Those terms are irrelevant. They're just qualifiers which we made up. We want to make judgments but what is, is. There is no better. No worse.

Allison's family was polite, distant and distracted at the funeral. I didn't give them any reason to behave differently towards me. There was no way I could tell them what Allison meant to me. I'm not even certain I've figured that out myself. I am grieving. I have no right to be grieving. I have every right to be grieving.

We never get notice that the last time is the last time. I had a job in college where they would send out a memo when we were going to have a fire drill. Just to let you know, Friday at 10am, there will be a fire drill. Please evacuate the building accordingly. I always though that sort of defeated the purpose. I mean, a real fire probably isn't going to send a memo.

The same is true about endings. We don't get a memo. No matter what we say or how we act, our brains always embrace the hope of an infinite future. We only see the end in retrospect. Even when we precipitate an ending or participate in an ending, it often seems surreal or not what we'd envisioned.

Maybe I should have stayed with her that night. Would it have made a difference? Would have it just postponed the inevitable? I don't know. I will never know and I will have to live with that not knowing forever.

Allison and I were having an affair. We met at a photography exhibit. She was looking some black and white pictures of the seashore. I was showing photos I'd taken of Victorian houses. She looked beautiful and nervous all at once. I knew she didn't have work in the exhibit, so I was intrigued. I couldn't imagine what she might have to look nervous about. I'm always attracted to women I can't quite figure out. I want to be challenged somehow.

I look at people and try to determine their backstory just based on appearances. Maybe you will think this is shallow or judgmental. Perhaps it is. After all, deducing a person's story just by looking at them, reduces them down solely to my own perceptions. It discounts their history and their personal tragedies. It does not honor their epiphanies or their moments of insight. But I am surprisingly good at it. I am right more often than not. When I find I am right, I often lose interest. When I can't immediately figure people out, I go talk to them. I'm intrigued.

I walked up and asked her if she was a photographer. It was such a throw away line. It didn't have any more sincerity than "Hey baby, what's your sign?" or "come here often?" It was just an in. A way to talk to her.

"Yes, well no. Well I'm not a professional or anything," she said and laughed uncomfortably.

" I take some pictures here and there just for fun," she stammered. She tucked a strand of hair behind her ear and jostled her champagne flute, spilling a little. The overall effect should have made her seem pathetic but in fact it was so endearing, I was smitten.

That's such an old fashioned word but it's the word that pops into my head when I remember that night. Attraction is such a fickle thing. It takes so many factors into account most of which, we aren't even fully conscious of. Who even knows why we are enamored of the people and things we are?

We chatted for a bit. I encouraged her to apply for the photography fellowship right off the bat. I didn't know if she had any talent but truly I just wanted to spend some more time with her. She was goregeous. She had long blonde hair with natural highlights like she spent every day at the beach. She had light brown eyes. She wasn't pretty in a Barbie doll, princess sort of way, more like a competent, intelligent surfer girl.

Anyway, it's my fellowship. It's my money. So there is no organizing committee. There is no board. She applied and I accepted her application with delight. In my defense, I did teach her some things about photography. She had a good eye but needed to learn technique. She liked different perspectives on everyday objects, hyper focusing or looking at things from odd angles. I taught her a few things about focus and lighting, that was all.

She did a whole series of black and white photographs of ordinary things which I felt were good enough to exhibit and we did. I own a gallery, so I can do these things. Her whole family and several friends came out to support her. In hindsight, I can tell you she was amazingly anxious about the whole thing. At the time, I had no idea why she seemed nervous. Now, I think she thought she wasn't good enough somehow. She never came out and said it.

But I can look back on things she almost said or things she sort of said and piece it together. If I could have had such insight at the end, maybe things would be different today. Maybe she felt that kind of anxiety about her whole life, who knows? If she did, she took pains to hide it. She did it well. That kind of insight seldom comes through in the moment though.

I called her a few days after our first meeting. I asked her to dinner, ostensibly to talk more about the fellowship. But I was asking her out and I knew it. We talked. I flirted with her shamelessly. I poured on the charm. I knew she was married but I felt zero guilt. Sometimes, I think I had no acquaintance with guilt whatsoever until Allison died. Now I know guilt much more intimately than I would like to.

Did I love her? I don't know. I think I was beginning to, but I don't know that we had hope of any kind of a future together. Even if you took her drinking out of the picture, it was never going to work. She wasn't going to leave her husband and those girls. She still loved him, I think. Why was she with me me then? I don't know. I didn't want to know. Why should I feel guilty about that? I wasn't married. Those were *her* issues. If that makes me a selfish jerk then so be it.

Allison had an inner light that could blind you. She was amazing and passionate. New ideas seemed to catch fire in her soul and ignite her from within. But she had a darkness inside her too. The light was compelling. The darkness was frightening. At the end of our relationship (which I didn't really know was the end) I was never sure which one I would get.

She was married. Initially, I didn't have to look for too much meaning. I had the luxury of not having to define anything. Maybe I wouldn't even have been interested if she'd really been available.

No, she didn't tell me why she felt compelled to cheat on a man she'd been with for years. And I never asked her. What kind of insights might she have given me if I had asked? Would she have told me? Did she even know herself? Or would she have told me to shut up and kissed me until I did? I have so many questions now. I don't know why I didn't think to ask any of them before but you never know you are out of time until you are.

Sometimes you don't even realize it until it's way past being too late.

She was like no one I'd ever met. She was vivascious. She had an energy that made you want to be a part of whatever she was doing. We were together (as much as we actually were together) for a little over a year. Her husband was proud of her for winning the fellowship. I don't know if he was woefully naive or just trusting. Maybe Allison had never given him a reason not to trust her before. She was someone you wanted to trust.

At first, the relationship was amazing and so much fun. She was such a free spirit. When things started to change, I didn't even notice right away. When I did, I couldn't seem to disengage. Her drinking began to irritate me. By irritate, I really mean frighten, but irritation seemed easier to deal with. Anger felt a hell of a lot better than worry.

She'd had a glass of champagne in her hand at the photography exhibit where we met but so did lots of people. I had no idea that alcohol was a problem for her. It occurs to me that it really wasn't a problem until more recently. By more recently, I mean after we met. This is something I don't want to look at too closely. There's more culpability for me there and I don't want it. It wasn't my job to fix her or save her.

When we were together, she'd bring a bottle of wine. As time went by, she drink the whole bottle by herself. Eventually a second bottle appeared. On that last night, she was actually working on a third. She said drinking made Dave and the girls nervous and she didn't feel like she could do it at home or when she was out with them. She said she felt liberated around me. In this case, I wish she'd been more inhibited.

It wasn't that she was a super obnoxious drunk. She didn't get angry or violent or sulky or morose. But she was different when she drank. It sounds weird but one of the things I liked best about Allison was the way she was fiercely protective of the people she loved. She loved her girls, her friends and even her husband, I think. But when she drank, it seemed like she stopped caring. Sober, she wanted to save the world. Drunk, it felt like she cared only about herself. That isn't quite right either. Drunk, Allison didn't seem to care about anything at all. It was terrifying.

Allison shone with this inner light which sounds trite and overdone but it wasn't really. Yet when she drank, that light was dimmed somehow. It was like putting a blanket over a flashlight. The light was still there but it was so dim and muffled, you couldn't even really see the source.

Usually, we met up at my apartment in the city, Her house was about a half an hour away. It wasn't an unreasonable drive. Anyway, that night, we'd arranged to meet at a local motel. It was the ultimate cheating cliché. I gave her some line about it feeling more exciting and forbidden.

It was a lie though. My sister and my nephew were coming later in the week for the Fourth of July holiday. Somehow it felt wrong to have Allison in my apartment just before they came to visit, I know, I'm a hypocrite. It's okay to have an affair with a married woman and to sleep with her in a cheap motel but not okay to leave traces of her around your family. How can you care about someone, maybe even love them, be fascinated by them, find them attractive and deeply arousing and still be a little bit ashamed of them at the same time? I wasn't proud of it but there it was.

Allison got there before me that night. She was already really drunk. I walked through the door and she kissed me sloppily and started tugging on my clothes. Crazy sex with an attractive drunk woman was every guy's dream, right? Except I couldn't. She was a hot mess and I was repulsed.

I should have put her to bed and stayed with her. I should have called her husband. I should have brought her back to my place. I should have tried to get her some help or held her and talked it out or taken her car keys. I could have done any number of things which might have caused a different outcome. But I didn't.

I lost my temper. I called her some names which I regret. I told her we were done. I swear I hadn't been planning on breaking it off when I walked through that door. Yes, I'd thought about it. I knew she and I were a lost cause for all sorts of reasons. Her drinking was only one of those reasons. I had no idea that I would actually do it. I lost my temper. I lost my mind. I said unkind things and walked away. You never know the last time is the last time.

Allison was one of the smartest people I have ever met. I was certain she'd sleep it off and go home the next morning with some excuse Dave would be sure to believe. I had no idea she would try to drive home and wind up dead in a pond.

Could I have prevented what happened? Could I have acted like a more decent human being? If I really did love her would that have been enough to save her? I don't know. I don't know.

From Allison's "Things Fall Apart" Playlist
1)Hurt-Johnny Cash
2)Nobody Home-Pink Floyd
3)If I Had a Heart-Fever Ray
4)Humpty Dumpty-Aimee Mann
5)You Know I'm No Good-Amy Winehouse
6)Criminal-Fiona Apple
7)Lost Cause-Beck
8)Lost!-Coldplay
9)Blue Monday-New Order
10)Nothing Else Matters-Metallica

From Allison's Photography Show, September 2013

"You only might have known
No one else had such wisdom
Such insight
Or knew me so well."
T.F. Forester

Jenna
July
One week after the accident

How can my mom be dead? How is that even possible? It's just a nightmare It has to be. Any time now, I'll wake up and my mom will ask me about last semester's grades and ask if I'm saving money for next semester (or spending it all on clothes and shoes and coffee and pizza and God knows what else.) She will smooth my hair like she did when I was little and I swear I won't hate it ever again. I promise I will never again resent it when she tries to take care of me because I'm 19 and in college and I'm an adult. She can take care of me all she wants.

I'm 19 years old and the first funeral I've ever been to was my mom's. That feels so unfair. It all feels unfair actually. I might drown in the unfairness of it all. But I can't. I have to keep going, even if I'm only treading water.

I feel like mom was a little weird when I came home at the beginning of the summer. She was distant somehow, like maybe she had a secret. She complained of headaches a lot. And once or twice, when she got home from her photography class, I could have sworn she smelled like alcohol.

My college dorm was actually a suite. There were four double rooms around a shared common area. I knew people who had issues with their roomates or other suitemates but I got along famously with most of mine.

Last fall, I had a suite mate named Rachel. Rachel was a big drinker. It was college though and although some people were really straight edge, lots of people were drinking, including me. But Rachel seemed different than the rest of us somehow. We had the vague idea that maybe Rachel had a problem although none of us in the dorm had any inkling of how we might help her. Or if we should even try to help her. Wasn't college all about doing your own thing? Was Rachael's drinking really any of our business? She kind of kept to herself. She didn't usually want to go out with us, preferring to drink in the dorm by herself.

After a few of her refusals of our invitations, we stopped asking her. We didn't know her very well and it didn't seem like she wanted us to. After Thanksgiving break, Rachel didn't come back. Nobody knew for sure what had happened but there were rumors that she had gotten alcohol poisoning one night and wound up in rehab. We didn't see her again.

Somehow, I kept associating Rachel with my mom. It didn't make any sense to me. I didn't understand why. My mom was passionate, creative and always totally together. Yet I thought I'd seen a look in her eyes that I'd also seen in Rachel's. Was there a certain "look" people got when they were drinking too much? People could look haunted for a whole variety of reasons. I wondered if my mom was drinking though. But what if she was? I mean, she was an adult. She could do what she wanted but it felt wrong somehow. Could I have even asked her about it? It would have been so weird to ask "Mom, do you have a drinking problem?" I'm the 19-year old college student. It seems like she should be asking me that.

Besides, maybe I was just being paranoid and thinking she was all secretive because I came home with a secret myself. Mom was going to be around for the long weekend and I was finally going to talk to her about it. She was so busy lately. She worked part time and did all of her photography stuff and stuff with Charlotte and April's school. In fact, as scared as I was, she was the *only* person I wanted to talk to about it right now.

My friends would be weird about it. April is so angry all the time and Charlotte is too young to understand it. My dad is great but he wouldn't get it. Pretty soon, it's going to be obvious and I won't have any choice but to talk about it though.

Jason and I had been inseparable the whole school year. We'd met in the dining hall on the second day of classes. We were both freshmen and both a little overwhelmed. Growing up, my sisters and I had always heard the story of how Mom and Dad met in college. It was romantic although it induced eye-rolling when we were younger. Secretly, though, I thought if it worked for them, it was a good omen that I met Jason that way.

We had done everything together for months. Everything. *Everything.* I hadn't thought he'd be overjoyed at the news that I was pregnant but I didn't expect him to bail. I wasn't overjoyed myself at the news that I was pregnant but it was what it was.

I looked for a good way and time to tell him. I wasn't naive enough to think it should necessarily be a romantic moment but I thought it should at least be marked in some way as *significant.* After all, this was the rest of our lives we were talking about.

Usually, we just ate in the college cafeteria or ocassionally ordered pizza but we actually made plans to go out to dinner at a nice restaurant off campus. I figured that would be perfect. We'd be happy and relaxed and in a neutral place. We'd be able to focus on each other. Talk about our hopes and fears and blah, blah, blah.

When it came time to go though, Jason didn't want to. He said he was broke. I offered to pay but he said he really just didn't feel like going. We walked to the campus store and got smoothies instead. On the way back, I sat on a bench. Despite the fact that the calendar had said it was spring for weeks, the sky had remained grey and surly, continuing to spit snow here and there. That day though, it was finally warm and sunny.

"What are you doing?" he complained.

I hadn't actually thought about anything other than resting a bit when I sat down. I didn't know if it was the stress of the semester or the pregnancy but I was really tired.

"I just wanted to feel the sun on my face," I said defensively.

He checked the time on his phone and looked annoyed but said nothing. He didn't sit down either.
I asked him to then.

"I have something to tell you," I said.

He seemed agreived but he reluctantly sat on the bench with me.

"I'm pregnant," I blurted out. None of this was going the way I'd envisioned it.

"You're sure?" he asked.

There wasn't a lot of compassion or concern in those two words. In fact, the subtext I heard in my head was "Really? You're a woman who loses her keys three times a week. I'm not really sure that I can trust you to know this sort of thing for certain.

"Yes," I said simply.

He didn't say anything. I didn't think I could feel worse but in a moment, I totally did.

"I love you," I said.

We hadn't exchanged "I loves yous" before and we didn't then either.

He just sat there, not responding and not looking at me. I felt panic start to rise up in me. I quelled it with anger.

"Can you please just say something? Anything at all?" I asked, my voice rising.

Instead of contrition or comfort, though, he turned it around, like he was the victim.

"Jeez, Jenna, give me a break. It's a lot to take in. And you really picked a lousy time to dump this on me."

Jason finished his last final two days before I finished mine. He loaded his stuff into his car and we said goodbye on a Tuesday. I was still pained by his reaction to the news of my pregnancy but I was determined not to push my luck. We hadn't talked about it since the afternoon on the bench. Things had started to feel normal between us again. I clung to that.

"I won't call you tomorrow," he said "To give you some space to study."

I appreciated it. My last final on Thursday was in Statistics which I had struggled with all semester. His not calling seemed like a considerate thing at that point.

"Call me on Thursday, when you get home," he added cheerfully and kissed me quickly.

We each live about an hour from the college but in different directions. I figured we might not see each other all the time over the summer, especially since we were both going to be working. But I imagined we'd manage a night during the week and some weekends.

He didn't mention the baby when he left and neither did I. I assumed he was absorbing the information. Processing. Figuring out what to do. I assumed we'd have plenty of time to discuss what happened next.

We see the things we want to see. We purposefully ignore things which should set off alarm bells in our heads. We pretend we don't hurt. We assume maybe we're not worthy of being treated better. What's that old saying? Denial is not just a river in Egypt.

I called him on Thursday night like he'd asked. He didn't answer. I called four times in the next couple of hours and hung up. The fifth time, I even left a message, which I never do.

"What's wrong with leaving a message?" Dad always asks. But leaving a message is annoying. Nobody even does that anymore.

"Um, hi Jason. It's me. You asked me to call, so I'm calling. Um, so yeah, I guess I'll talk to you later."

It was super awkward. It's always super awkward. This is why nobody wants to leave messages. I told myself he'd forgotten to charge his phone or lost it somewhere. I messaged him on Facebook. Then I went to take a shower. I made myself walk away. Although if he didn't have his phone, he probably wasn't going to check Facebook. But I was starting to feel desperate. Logic was beyond me at that point. We've gotten so used to being able to communicate with people instantly. It's hard not to feel impatient when that doesn't work. Mom and Dad talk about life without cell phones but I can't even picture it. It seems like the dark ages or something. When I got out of the shower, I looked at Messenger. I had been blocked.

He's just gone. He doesn't take my calls. He doesn't respond to my texts. Ghosting they call it. I feel like I might be the ghost. I feel sort of needy and desperate but I'm trying hard not to be *that* girl. Those girls always seemed awful to me. I'm talking about those clingy girls who can't be without a boyfriend. I've always looked down on those women who needed all of a guy's attention all of the time or who got jealous of his friends. Now, I was one of them.

My mom would have understood. She would have had something comforting to say, then she would have helped me figure out what to do next. I mean, I know what I'm going to do. I'm going to have the baby. I'm going to be a mother. I try hard not to judge other people's choices but I know what I'm capable of. So, yeah, I've decided, but it would still be great to hear mom say she thought I was doing the right thing. To hear her say how she would be supportive because she was ALWAYS supportive. I wanted to hear her thoughts and ideas.

How can I possibly become a mother when my own mother is gone?

*"Your anger and your sadness
are so intertwined, so completely
enmeshed
You cannot know
They are one and the same."*
T.F. Forester

April
July
Twelve days after the accident

Screw her. Yeah, I said it and I don't feel bad. Screw her for dying and for being so involved in her photography and with that stupid photography teacher. Yeah, I knew about him. She didn't know I knew, but I did. Jenna thinks mom could do no wrong and Charlotte is too young to understand anything but I know lots of things.

The reason I know about him is because of Elise. Elise is my best friend. She lives next door. Elise doesn't know that she's the reason, because I didn't tell her, but I know because of her. She also doesn't know mom's secret. Elise would have mocked it. She would have made it somehow less than it was. I can picture her shrugging and saying "So your mom has a boyfriend? Lots of people cheat on their spouses. What's the big deal? Why do you care?"

I did care though. I thought it was huge and horrible. The knowledge hurt my heart. I didn't want anyone diminishing that. I didn't want it to hurt either but I didn't want anyone to make it less than it was if that makes any sense.

Anyway, Elise and I skipped school one day last spring. The department store in the mall was giving away makeup samples – good stuff, not the cheap crap we sometimes steal from Walmart- and Elise said we had to go. I wear makeup sometimes but Elsie is a freak about it.

She makes videos about how to apply it and puts them on YouTube. Sometimes she has me film her. Some of her stuff is actually pretty cool – cats eyes and harlequins and all kinds of crap. I don't want to do that stuff myself but I guess it's kind of neat that she does. I like makeup okay but I don't have time for all that bullshit. If it takes more than five minutes to apply, I'm over it.

Anyway, the store that was giving away samples is in the mall in the city, not the boring, close to home mall, that mom used to bring me and Jenna and Charlotte to. Elise and I skipped school and took the train. Elise bought the tickets. She steals money from her dad, so she has money in her pocket all the time. I can't figure out if he's too dumb to notice or he just ignores it because he feels bad because she doesn't have a mom. Elise's mom walked out years ago. Guess what? I don't have a mom either anymore.

Elise got a few lipstick samples but then the lady behind the counter was all like "How old are you anyway?" and "Why aren't you in school?" and she wouldn't give her anything else and we bailed. I was just standing there, feeling uncomfortable, absolutely certain that we were going to get caught but pretending I was all cool and didn't care. I do that a lot. I pretend I don't care. Sometimes I even believe it myself for a few minutes. Fake it 'til you make it right?

We had to walk back to the train. Elise was going on about makeup and being all annoyed that she didn't get some specific metallic eye-shadow that she really wanted as a sample because it actually cost like $30 and you couldn't shoplift from those mall makeup counters like you could at Walmart. I was sort of half listening. I do this with Elise a lot which is probably awful because she's my best friend. But she goes off on these tangents that only she really cares about. I listen enough so that I can respond if it seems like she needs my response. Most of the time, she doesn't.

Sometimes I feel like I care about all the wrong things. Life might be a lot easier if I could get all amped up about clothes or makeup instead of feeling like I'm always on the edge of some existential, over thinking crisis. So, was sort of half listening to Elise when I saw them across the street.

I recognized the guy from the gallery where Mom had showed her photographs. I was really proud of her that night but I didn't know how to tell her, so I didn't. Moms are supposed to be proud of their kids. It's in the job description. But it's just weird when it's the other way round.

They were just walking at first. I pulled up the hood on my jacket and tried to make myself small so Mom wouldn't see me. But she was oblivious. She seemed totally wrapped up in whatever the guy was saying. Then the dude pushed her up against the wall and stuck his tongue down his throat.

I stopped dead. I couldn't help it. I just stared. At first I thought maybe mom was being assaulted by this guy but she was totally participating. That idea was more horrifying than the thought of her being attacked. Elise was rambling on and kept walking for a while, not noticing that I'd stopped. Finally she figured it out and asked me what the hell was my problem and I told her I saw a homeless guy pee on the sidewalk. She laughed, which I wanted her to. I laughed too, but something twisted and hot seared through my insides.

So screw her. Mom used to do all kinds of things with us when we were little. We went off on adventures together. She took pictures but it was always at places she thought we might find interesting too. And okay, I'll give her this, she still sort of tried to do stuff with us. Honestly sometimes I just didn't want to do stuff with my mom, so that's on me. But she'd been different the last couple of years too. Was it because of that guy? I dunno. She was distracted. She was sad in some way she didn't express maybe. But she was the mom. She didn't get to be sad while she still had us to take care of.

I hate her for dying and leaving us.

From Allison's "Things Fall Apart" Playlist
    11) Everything Zen-Bush
    12) December-Collective Soul
    13) Loser-Beck
    14) Creep-Radiohead
    15) Time To Pretend-MGMT

from Allison's photography show, September 2013

"Your sadness is silent and gut wrenching
And somehow
Takes on a life of its very own."
T.F. Forester

Charlotte
July
Nine days after the accident

Jenna and April still think I'm a baby. I suppose I get it. Jenna was six when I was born and already going to school. April was in preschool. Now Jenna's in college and April's in high school and I've only just started middle school.

I'm quiet. I observe. I notice things and I think about them. Everything I think doesn't automatically fall out of my mouth unlike some people. I don't even always feel comfortable around people my own age. I understand things people think I shouldn't be able to. Sometimes I just know things. Mom always said I was an old soul. I Googled it and maybe she's right. Or she *was* right because I'm still trying to process that everything about mom is in the past tense now.

I know that Jenna or April is pregnant. I found the pee stick in the upstairs trash. My money is on Jenna. She had a boyfriend at college and they were all hot and heavy for a while. I don't know if it's still on though. Jenna talked about him a lot when she was home on spring break but she hasn't said much about him since she's been home for the summer. I don't know if I should ask her about it or not.

It could be April too but I don't think so. April talks a good game. She tries to seem like a bad girl. I don't think she really is a bad girl. What makes a bad girl anyway? I feel like all those definitions are all outdated, like they came from the 1950's or something. What I really think, is that April uses her "I could care less" persona to cover some pretty serious anxiety. She was always anxious when we were little. I don't think that just went away. I think she just covers it better now. April used to talk to me about stuff. Now she doesn't.

Jenna and Dad are lost. April is angry but then April is *always* angry these days. Me, I'm just sad, I don't even know what to do with so much sadness.

I can remember learning about the pilgrims and the Mayflower in social studies last year. The teacher had talked about how tiny the ship actually was and how awful the conditions were for the people aboard because they were all crammed in together. He had talked about sea sickness. He said when you were sea sick, the first day was awful because you felt like you were going to die. He said the second day was worse because you knew you were going to die. But, he said, the third day was the worst of all because you knew you weren't going to die.

I don't know if his description was from personal experience or he was quoting something he'd read but that description has stayed with me. It almost felt that way with grief, I thought. I wasn't feeling suicidal and I didn't want to die but the knowledge that I was going to have to live through feeling so completely awful was painful.

I found a journal of mom's. It was wedged behind the washing machine in the laundry room. I threw a load into the washer a little too enthusiastically and one of my favorite socks went right over the back of the washer. I went to retrieve it and there was a generic looking black and white composition book filled with Mom's neat printing, I've started to read it. I'm spacing it out. I read a little bit at a time, as if somehow by not rushing through it, I could hang onto her a little longer. I haven't shared it with anyone. I don't know if I will. I know that I should but it's really sad. I'm not sure it would make anyone feel better.

I didn't know Mom was so sad. I didn't know how *wrong* things had gotten for her. I don't know how I could have helped her if I had. None of us could have helped her, I don't think. Still, I wish we'd known. Mom was the one person who always seemed to have it all together even when everybody else was a hot mess. Yet reading her journal, I see that it wasn't true. It makes me wonder what else in my life isn't true.

"I look backwards and criticize myself
'What did my foolish heart know of love?'
I was naive
Yet we know what we know
We cannot know some things until we are
ready
And we may never be ready
In ten years, I will look back and ask
'What did my foolish heart know of love?'
T.F. Forester

David
July
One week after the accident

Allison was the love of my life. That sounds like a stupid cliché but it's true, and I don't know how to say it in any other way. We met in college. I had a work study job in the tutoring center, and she had an F in algebra. She walked into the tutoring center one drizzly, Wednesday November afternoon, and I was struck. I guess that's a weird way to say it, but that's how it felt. Obviously, she didn't hit me physically, but something inside me was knocked flat. In that moment, I knew I'd never be the same. It felt like a kick in the solar plexus. It wasn't painful. It just knocked the wind out of me both physically and metaphorically. It was love at first sight. Another cliché.

I wish I had better words to describe what she meant to me or perhaps some way of communicating that didn't use words at all. When I try to put those feelings into words, they don't nearly convey what I want them to. Would that I could express it through scent, or music, or taste like some odd synesthesia.

I couldn't *not* love her. I had never *not* loved her. Yet the fact that she loved me back seemed like a gift from God, or the universe, or whatever you want to call it. How had I managed to be so lucky? I didn't deserve her, I was certain. I never stopped believing that, even after two decades of marriage. Even when things got bumpy. Perhaps especially when things got bumpy.

Allison hadn't seemed happy for the last few months of her life. I don't know why but then I often didn't know the whys of Allison. Loving her all those years didn't necessarily give me insight into what was going on in her head. She was both a "wear her heart on her sleeve" kind of person and incredibly complicated all at the same time. She was always the intuitive, insightful one and she knew lots of things about people.

I should have asked her directly what was wrong. There were a bunch of times when I almost did but I kept expecting that she would just tell me. She always had before. It wasn't like her to keep it to herself if she was miserable. So I kept thinking, "Well maybe it's just me. Maybe she's not really unhappy or "off" even though, deep down, I knew well enough that she was. We see the things we want to see, I guess. We refuse to see the things which frighten us or make us uncomfortable.

Allison was an amazingly devoted mother. I felt like she always instinctively knew what to do for the girls. From croup to heartbreak and from colic to bad teachers, she could always say the right things to make it better for them. I love my girls. They mean the world to me. Yet, if push comes to shove, I'm not sure I trust myself to do right by them. Oh, I will try. Honestly and sincerely. But I'm sure I'll do the wrong thing. I'll screw it up somehow. Allison always seemed to do the right things for them.

As I'm thinking this now, I'm realizing that push actually *has* come to shove. I'm never going to have a better opportunity to step up (or screw up) than this. Oh Allison, I'm almost angry that you're not here when I need you the most. Almost angry but not quite. Angry might be better, I think, instead of just lost. I am so very lost.

"There can be no prideful 'I told you so'
When our worst fears
Turn out to be justified."
T.F. Forester

Cindy
July
Fifteen days after the accident

I asked her outright about a month before the accident.

I said, "Baby, are you drinking?"

My mama drank. My brothers are both alcoholics. I know what it looks like. I told her from the time she was ten years old that she would have to be careful. This disease runs in our family, I said. It's a disease but you still have to think carefully about your choices. If you start, you may not be able to stop.

There was trouble here and there when she was a teenager. Those years were rough. I worried that it was the start of something bad. Something she wouldn't be able to control. But when she met David in college, she calmed down. She might have occasionally had a glass of wine, but I never saw her drunk after that.

Until a few months ago.

Baby, are you drinking?

When she was in high school, she would deny it vehemently. Even if she came home drunk, Even after I found bottles in her dresser drawers or in her car. She would always deny it.

"I don't drink, mom." or "Those aren't mine." She always had some denial at the ready. I didn't really believe them. She didn't believe that I believed them. But I would back off. I would remind her to be careful. I would advise her to remember the family history. She would humor me and assure me that she was fine and making good choices until the next incident.

She was basically a good kid. Her grades were decent. She had a lot of friends. She never got arrested. Thank God she never got into real trouble. She never got hurt and she never hurt anyone else. Thank, God.

But when I asked her a few months ago, she just laughed like a loon. "I only drink by myself or with friends," she joked, like it was the funniest thing in the world.

It scared me. I could deal with her denials. I understood those. She had been making them forever but she was so cavalier about it this time. So flippant. Her non-denial felt wrong to me. I thought she was in trouble and I didn't know how to help her. I wanted to mother her even though she was a mother herself.

From Allison's Photography Show, September 2013

*"You cannot see the light
without having gone first through the
darkness
Yin and yang and all that
In what terrible balance we hang."
T.F. Forester*

Sarah
July
Twenty-three days after the accident

Everyone wanted to stand in Allison's light. She never used that to her advantage. She never used that light to manipulate people. I'm not even sure she understood how brightly she shone. Complete strangers would engage her in conversation all of the time. At the store. In the doctor's office. In parking lots. Allison never started these conversations. But she always participated in them willingly. She always made those random strangers feel like she really heard them. Allison could make you feel that whatever you had to say was important. She really listened where most people appeared distracted or annoyed.

I met Allison in junior high. She was editor of the school paper and she was protesting a sign. The sign in question lit up and you could type your text in so it displayed on the screen. The school used it to remind us about the homecoming dance or cheer leading tryouts and that sort of stuff. Allison called it the funky, flaming, flashing sign. She *hated* that sign. She wrote editorials for the paper. She met with the principal. She talked to anybody who would listen about it. She argued that the school needed new windows. She argued that when she sat in her Latin class, chunks of the ceiling would fall onto her desk as students worked in a ceramics class in the art room directly above. She cited outdated textbooks and an elderly heating system. She had a whole list of things she felt the school needed more than it needed this sign.

It turned out that the sign had been donated or something. The school hadn't actually purchased it. Allison didn't give up and didn't loathe it any less. She then argued that it should be sold then to fund something more useful for the school.

Other people (like me for example) might have just been seen as malcontents or complainers. But everybody loved Allison. If anything, they loved her even more for hating the sign. Even the principal, who I suspect got the brunt of Allison's annoyance, called her "energetic" and "spirited" and said there should be more students like her involved in making the school a better place.

I was shy and new to the school and completely blown away when she chose to sit next to me at lunch one day. She introduced herself and asked me if I'd seen the sign. I said I'd noticed it. She asked me if the'd had anything like it at my old school. I said no.

"See?" she asked as if my old school not having a similar sign completely justified her outrage. She might have walked away then, confident in her convictions. But she choose to keep sitting with me not only that day but for days and years after that. Allison always had her "causes" but we talked about all sorts of other things too. We talked about mundane things like makeup and boys and deeper, important things like philosophy and the nature of the universe. We talked about everything.

From that day, until the day she died, I always thought I was getting way more out of our relationship than she was. I was honored to be her friend, even when she made me crazy which she sometimes did. I could not imagine life without her. I still can't.

The thing about Allison was that she was amazing but she didn't know it. If you told her, she brushed it off like she didn't believe it. I don't think it was just humility on her part; she really didn't believe it. She would laugh off any accusations of greatness. She would insist that she was just like everybody else. She wasn't though.

Three of her ex-boyfriends from high school showed up at her funeral. These were guys she had broken up with years and years before. Allison had never been the dumpee. She was always the dumper. Yet she did it in a way that let guys know that she was all devastated about it too. It was just the way it had to be. These guys awkwardly shook hands with David at the funeral. They hugged me even more awkwardly. After all, I'd known them all back in the day.

Every single one of them looked like they had just lost Allison. I guess in a way they had, even though none of them had seen her in years. Who knew what kind of hurts they still harbored in their hearts? But you didn't forget Allison. If she was stuck in your heart, she was probably going to be stuck there forever.

Allison had a way of branding herself onto people. It wasn't done in a heavy-handed way. I don't even think she knew she did it. But people always wanted to be able to say that they knew her. That they had loved her or that in even in some small way, she had loved them. Being loved by Allison was a beautiful thing.

*"How can I explain myself to you
When I understand nothing myself?"*
T.F. Forester

From Allison's Journal
February 2014
Five months before the accident

    I haven't talked to Sarah or mom about Adam. I feel like they wouldn't understand. I feel like *I* don't understand, so how could I possibly explain it to someone else? It's not precisely that David isn't fulfilling my needs. If I were honest and just asked for things, I'm sure we would work it out. He would be accommodating. He always has been. Except that I'm not even sure what my needs even really are. How do you explain that something is missing when that something isn't anything you can even make tangible in your own brain? And maybe it isn't David himself or David and I at all.

    Maybe something is missing from me. That seems more likely actually. The fault is mine. I am not enough in some way. I just don't know where the lack is or how I might improve it. I should just walk away from Adam. David and I have been married for years. Isn't that worth investing my time into fixing? Why can't I seem to muster the energy to *want* to fix it? I feel like regardless of the choices I make (or do not make) there is no world in which this ends well. For any of us.

"Your sad, distracted heart
Speaks her name
Over and over
Like a mantra
or a curse
If you would but listen."
T.F. Forester

Adam
August
One month after the accident

I'm out with a woman I've been on several dates with now. She's pretty. She's smart. She's animatedly telling me about something she did at her job today, doing something or other with special education. There's a pause and I can see she's waiting for me to respond in some way. Then it hits me; not only have I not been listening, I don't care.

I've dated a lot of women. It's true, I've never really settled down. I've never been married or engaged or even cohabited with a woman but dammit, I've always been a good boyfriend. I'm courteous. I'm considerate. I have a bit of a reputation as, I don't know, a playboy maybe? Is that term so dated it doesn't even make sense anymore? At any rate, I've annoyed a few women by not wanting more but I've always been a basically nice guy. I listen when women talk.

So, I apologize to the woman I'm with and I mean it. I make some excuse about not feeling well, which honestly, I'm not. I stay present and give her my full attention for the rest of the day. She accepts my apology.

Later, when I'm by myself, I wonder what's wrong with me. But I really don't have to wonder. I know what's wrong with me. Allison is wrong with me. Allison who drank too much and cheated on her husband with me and told lies to her daughters. Allison who made me angry and sad and guilty and who I thought I was happy to be done with.

Those negative feelings are all truth of some sort. But they aren't the only truth. The real truth of any situation is usually much more complicated than just one type of feeling. And my truth about Allison is no different. Yes, she made me angry and sad and guilty but she also made me feel alive and sometimes joyful and even though she never said "I love you", I felt loved with her.

Then the words pop into my head, like they were written out on a billboard in bright neon:

I was in love with her. I handed her my heart. Willingly and without thought for the consequences. I hadn't been willing to see the truth of it but that didn't make it any less true. As soon as I know this, I want to unknow it, to take it back somehow. I don't want to be in love with Allison. I don't want to finally know this only after she is gone and I have said unkind things. It's too much. My heart feels like it shatters.

"Such sadness
When your expectations
And your reality
Fail to compromise
Or even come close enough together
As to make any sense."
T.F. Forester

Jenna
July
19 days after the accident

Two weeks after mom's funeral, Jason finally answers one of my calls. A woman who was braver or smarter or somehow less lost would have stopped calling after being blocked on Facebook. My mom would have probably been that braver smarter woman but I am not. I have called him at least once a day since the end of the semester. It's pathetic and I loathe myself for it but I was incapable of stopping myself.

My heart does a little leap at the sound of his voice. My joy lasts only a fraction of a second though. When I hear his tone, I know that the conversation is not going to be one I'm going to enjoy.

"Jenna," he says. I can almost hear him shaking his head in dismay over the phone.

"Jason," I begin. I want at least a chance to tell him something. I want to talk about my feelings. I want to talk about the baby. I want to convey my sense of hurt and betrayal. I want to still love him. I want him to still love me if he ever did. I want to question his behavior. I want to be able to say anything at all but he cuts me off.

"Jenna," he repeats. He says my name in a tone you might use with a uncooperative toddler or a misbehaving pet and I hate the way it sounds.

"You need to stop calling me. We're over. I won't be returning to school next semester and you and I are done talking."

"The baby," I manage to get out but I'm talking to the dial tone.

Mom would know what to do. Mom would know what to do. That thought plays in an endless loop in my head.

Mom and I never had a complicated relationship like she did with April or grandma. We didn't really butt heads or have fights or conflict. She loved me and took care of me and I took her for granted. It had never occurred to me to think that she wouldn't be here. I never once thought that I might lose her before I was ready. Yet, I could have been sixty and she eighty and I probably still wouldn't have been ready. But I'll never know.

I have to tell Dad and my sisters that I'm pregnant. I'll have to do it all by myself. Mom would have supported me. She would have been on my side. She always was. It's not that I think the rest of my family will disown me or anything but Mom would have known what to do.

"Forget going along to get along
I want to see your truth.
Your brave, honest, messy, ugly,
complicated truth."
T.F. Forester

April
August
33 days after the accident

"You're going to be an auntie!" Jenna announced.

She was so fake cheerful, I wanted to vomit. I know she's still heartbroken about mom. She's being inauthentic and a hypocrite and I hate it. Jenna accuses me of complaining sometimes but Jenna goes too far in the opposite direction. She always pretends everything is okay, even when it isn't. Jenna could be bleeding to death on the floor and she'd still say, "I'm fine." When I called her on it, she started to cry and Dad gave me a look. He told me to be considerate of my sister's feelings and to apologize. I did but I didn't necessarily mean it. I was still mad.

Honestly, she can't really be happy about a baby right now. She'll have to drop out of college indefinitely. I'm not stupid. I know how this goes. Indefinitely often becomes forever. I can tell you right now, no boy is ever going to knock me up and cheat me out of an education. Why is it wrong for me to want her to acknowledge how she really feels?

I don't know which is even worse, the fact that Jenna is acting all happy about the baby or the fact that she expects me to be happy about it too. Like this is the best news ever. Like having a baby in the house is going to make me wildly ecstatic or something. I can tell Dad isn't sure how to react but he tries to seem happy about it. This is probably because Jenna is trying to seem happy about it. They feed off one another and nobody ends up telling the truth about their feelings. Who knows what Charlotte thinks? She's calm and she hugs Jenna but she doesn't say much.

It feels like all I have is anger. I am angry at Jenna for letting this happen and for trying to act like it's a good thing. I'm angry at Charlotte for being so calm all the time. It's like nothing ever bothers her. I'm angry at Dad for taking Jenna's side and not mine. But most of all, I'm angry at Mom. I'm angry because she could have smoothed it all out. She could have made it all right. For all of us. But she isn't here and won't be ever again. It sounds foolish because obviously, she couldn't control a car accident but I am so, so angry at her for not being here now.

"And it is both better and worse than you expected."
T.F. Forester

Charlotte
August
Thirty-four days after the accident

So, it's Jenna who is pregnant. I find myself relieved. I never really thought it was April but it did occur to me later that it could have been mom. I mean she was older but I don't think she was too old. She borrowed tampons from Jenna last month, so it was still possible. That would have been doubly sad, to know that she died while pregnant. That would have meant that we lost a brother or a sister too.

It would have been totally bizarre to have a new sibling as a teenager, I think, but still.

April is furious with Jenna. She feels Jenna is pretending to be happy. I can't quite get a read on how Jenna actually feels though. This isn't a dream come true for her, especially since she's had to drop out of school and she's told us that the boyfriend is a no show. Still, she seems determined to make the best of it. She will be a good mother, I think.

From Allison's Photography Show September 2013

"Your heart
So fragile, so fickle
So much frantic energy there
I could hold it in my hands
And still not fully know it."
T.F. Forester

David
August
42 days after the accident

For the first month or so, people were amazing. They brought food. They offered to help. It seemed like people were in the house all the time and that was good. I was alone at night after the girls went to bed though. Some of those nights were pretty bad. Some of them still are. My goal was to do so much during the day that I would just collapse in exhaustion when it ended. Sometimes that even worked. Sometimes not so much.

But now the funeral is done. The insurance stuff is dealt with. The house has been cleaned within an inch of it's life. Allison was many things; a loving wife, devoted mother, talented photographer but cleaning the house wasn't really her thing. I'm not saying she didn't pull her weight. She always did her fair share of the household stuff. Sometimes she did more than her fair share. But I don't think she took any pleasure in it. She did it because it needed to be done. Me, I like putting things in order. I enjoy knowing that I've put things away and tended to them in whatever way they needed tending. It's almost meditative for me. It calms me. But there just isn't anything else to tend to. I've done it all.

I haven't gotten rid of anything of Allison's. I merely put her things away. I hung her sweatshirt on the coatrack in the hall. I put her cell phone charger in the drawer in the kitchen. I know this likely says something about my state of mind but I refuse to deal with it right now. If her things are put away instead of discarded, she might come back. I know this isn't true. We had a funeral. She's gone and most of me knows it. The small part of me which wants to tend to things though, would like to continue to belive that it's all just a bad dream.

Maybe someday, some new projects will interest me. At the moment, though, I don't see myself being excited about anything ever again.

The police said Allison's blood alcohol level was .0.22 on the night of the accident. What the hell was that about? How could she have gotten behind the wheel of her car that drunk? Where had she been and what had she been doing that she had consumed so much alcohol?

That's well over the limit and drunk in a way I had NEVER seen her drunk. We drank in college sometimes. But she'd never seemed incapacitated in any way. She'd never blacked out. She could always remember what had happened the next day. She had always just seemed fun and flirty when she drank. Just more Allison if that makes any sense.

I know her mom felt she had a problem in high school. Cindy even asked me a few months ago if I thought Allison was having an issue now. But no. Ever since Jenna was born almost twenty years ago, I'd never seen Allison have more than the occasional glass of wine. I hadn't seen her drunk in years.

I can't wrap my brain around her loss. And I really can't wrap my brain around how it happened. What was she thinking? I feel like I'm desperate, frantic even, for some insight here. What was going on in her head and why didn't I know about it? If she was distressed, why hadn't she leaned on me for support? She always had before. She was complicated and I'm not going to pretend I knew every single thing about her (although she probably knew every single thing about me) but she had always confided in me. Told me things. I was her husband dammit. Why one month after her death am I completely at a loss to explain her behavior?

"Can you yet redeem yourself?
Cut yourself free from the net of guilt
In which you are hopelessly tangled
And thrashing like a tuna
Do you even deserve such redemption?"
T.F. Forester

Adam
September
Two months after the accident

This is the worst idea ever, I told myself. Yet, still, my feet moved up the sidewalk. I continued to walk despite the warning messages my brain was shouting.

I have gotten it into my head that I needed to talk to David. I need to tell him the truth about Allison and I. I don't understand where this came from. David and I have met exactly twice and one time was at Allison's funeral. It's not like he and I had been great friends and I felt I needed to make amends with him to preserve the friendship. We had nothing between us to preserve. Yet somehow, I felt I needed to make amends with him anyway.

I ring the bell and panic for a moment. What if one of her daughters answers the door or David isn't home? How do I possibly explain why I'm here? If I leave at this point, it's a pretty safe bet that I don't come back despite the compulsion to be here now. Then I probably torture myself some more. There is that guilt again. An emotion of which I was only peripherally aware for the first 35 years of my life. I'm not even sure that telling David the truth is going to dispel that guilt. I suspect maybe not.

David answers the door.

"Can I help you?" he asks.

He doesn't recognize me.

Like I said, I have only met him twice but he has clearly lost weight since the funeral. He has dark circles under his eyes. He looks hollow. Maybe even haunted. I consider fleeing but it's too late. I tell him my name and he processes this information for a few seconds.

"Oh yeah, the photography teacher," he finally says. "Come in."

Yes, the photography teacher, I think. But more than that. If he only knew. But he will know shortly. Unless I lose my nerve.

He has me sit on the couch and offers me a beer. I don't want one but feel I should accept it anyway. In the interest of camaraderie or whatever. What is wrong with me? I'm about to tell him I had a eighteen month long affair with his wife. I don't think my drinking his beer is going to allow that information be received in a better light. I'm screwing this up. It was never a good idea to begin with. But I am here. I have no alternative but to plunge ahead.

He waits. He can afford to. He didn't just appear in *my* living room.

"How are you doing?" I ask helplessly. It's a terrible opener. Who am I to ask? He doesn't even know me, really.

He shrugs. "You know..." he says and trails off and shakes his head.

And I do know. Sort of. But I also don't know at all. I loved Allison for a handful of months and didn't even admit it until after she was gone. This guy loved her for decades. He built a life with her. He fathered her children. So, yeah, I also really don't know.

"I wanted to talk to you about Allison," I say lamely.

He is patient. He gives me a look that seems to say "And...get to the point buddy" although he says nothing. Obviously, I want to talk about Allison. He and I have nothing else in common aside from being carbon based life forms.

"We were having an affair," I say simply.

He absorbs this. He appears surprised but only mildly so. He doesn't stand up and punch me in the face, although at this point that might be preferable to his silence. He takes his time, considering his words.

"Did you love her?" he finally asks. I don't know what I expected him to say at this juncture but this is not it.

I want to say I think so. I want to say yes but I didn't realize it. I want to say it was complicated. But he doesn't deserve any of my emotional drama. What's it to him?

"Yes," I say.

"Good," he says.

This takes me completely by surprise. So much so, that I can't even form the words for a coherent reply.

"She was worth loving," he adds, really looking at me for the first time.

I nod, unsure of the appropriate response here.

"I'd hate to see her with someone who was only using her," he continues. There is a slight challenge in this last. It's as if he's asking me directly if I was using her.

"I loved her," I say with more certainty.

"Good," he repeats. He pauses here and time spills out between us. I wrack my brain for something I can say which won't sound stupid or trite or patronizing or get me into more trouble than I'm already in. I come up empty.

Finally, he says "It's too late for either of us now though, isn't it?"

The question is rhetorical. I don't get to answer it although it's going to rattle around in my skull for a long time. He stands up and is already leading me to the door.

From Allison's "Things Fall Apart Playlist
    16) Desolation Row-Bob Dylan
    17) Smells Like Teen Spirit-Nirvana
    18) Mad World-Gary Jules
    19) How Soon Is Now?-The Smiths
    20) Bullet With Butterfly Wings-Smashing Pumpkins

"Examine your anger
Don't flee
Really look at it
And see
That it almost always covers up fear."
T.F. Forester

Sarah
September
Two months after the accident

I had been a little bit angry with Allison for several months before she died. She'd seen some of that anger but I hadn't really confronted her with it. I am so, so sorry about that now. If I had actually told her how I felt, maybe she could have really explained what was going on. My anger might have opened a dialogue.

I didn't like the affair. She had told me about it awkwardly last spring. It had been going on for several months at that point. I was torn between being happy she confided in me and annoyed that she hadn't told me sooner. Then immediately after she confided in me, I realized, I actually wasn't happy to know it. I was sorry to know her secret. I didn't want to meet Adam. I love Dave. He's been so good for Allison. He's loyal and faithful and just an all around good guy. He was always a stabilizing influence on Allison. The truth is, I've always had a little crush on him. I have never acted on it. Not only would it have felt wrong but I know that I could never, ever compete with Allison. She was a meteor shower. I was a flashlight's beam. I'm not being down on myself here. A flashlight can be a good thing. Flashlights have their uses. But a flashlight is never going to have the dazzle factor of a meteor shower.

One day, back in May, we were at the gallery where she had some of her photos exhibited. I had been to the opening reception the previous fall, along with the rest of the family. I had actually met Adam then, but of course I had no idea what he was to Allison at the point. I didn't even realize that he owned the gallery.

She dragged me there under the pretense of having to fix one of her photos. Something about a broken hanging wire, she said. In retrospect, I suppose it seems a little lame. Why did she need me with her for a minor repair? But we hadn't hung out much lately and I was happy just to be spending time with her.

Adam just happened to stop by the gallery while we were there. Except it was a setup. I wouldn't agree to meet him, so

Allison made sure that we "happened" to meet anyway. I was so angry. I didn't want to be complicit with her infidelity. I didn't want to meet Adam and I definitely didn't want to like him. The truth is, I didn't even really give the guy a chance. He didn't seem too bad. She really wanted us to get to know each other but I wasn't having it.

Now I ask, what if instead of just being angry, couldn't I have told her why? Couldn't I have told her what I was thinking or why I was scared for her (because all anger is really just a fear isn't it?) The truth was despite years of friendship, I still really wanted Allison's approval. I was okay with being mad at her but terrified that she might be angry with me.

"I miss you
In ways that I cannot even imagine
Drained of everything
But my love for you
A love which now
Has no place to go
It can neither be deferred nor transferred
And still I miss you"
T.F. Forester

Cindy
September
Two months after the accident

Parents aren't supposed to bury their children. It's not how it's supposed to work. Oh sure, intellectually, it's one of those things you know. People die and those people are often someone's child. But knowing it intellectually and having it visit your home and your heart are two very different things. It's like a traffic accident; until those blue flashing strobes are lighting up your car, it's sad but it's someone else's problem.

I will hold this family together. I love those girls with my whole heart. They may have lost their mom but they will have their grandma for as long as I live. In my own way, I love David too. Still, part of me feels like he should have seen this coming. How could he not know she was drinking so much? How did he not know what she was up to? Why did he let her spend all that time with that photography teacher?

He should have put his foot down. Now the girls are trying to rely on him but he just seems lost. Allison loved him, I know, but I always thought he was a little weak. Allison was such a free spirit. She was such a strong personality. You had to be a strong person to live with her and she needed someone to reign her in.

Yet part of me knows that this is my own sense of guilt talking. I couldn't keep her safe, so some irrational part of me, wants to be furious with him because he couldn't either. Can we really keep the people we love safe? Perhaps, to some extent. More so when they are younger. But when they are older, certainly by the time they are adults, there's not much we can do to protect them.

I think that we sometimes feel that if we just love them enough, the power of that love will be enough to insulate them from heartbreak or loss or that it might function like a magical talisman keeping them from all harm. It isn't true and I know it. I know that David could do no more for Allison through his love than I could through mine. And it hurts to even think about.

"It's the small, silly things
That I miss about you the most."
T.F. Forester

Charlotte
September
65 Days after the accident

April and I started school last week. Mom always took our pictures on the first day. Last year, April turned her back on mom just as she snapped the picture. Mom said it was okay but I could see she was hurt. This year, I bet April is sorry. I don't know. April doesn't really talk to me. April doesn't really talk to anyone except Elise from next door. I would talk to April. We used to play Barbies together while Jenna was at school. We used to get along. I kind of miss her but I don't even know how we could be friends again. It's not like I could just ask her.

Jenna talks to me now more than she ever did. She used to only interact with me in a bossy, oldest sister kind of way. She's lost a lot of that bossiness now. She's like that balloon that you fill with air but don't tie off, then you let it go. Jenna is deflated and sad. She pretends to be cheerful though. She acts like she's really happy about being pregnant although I don't know if she really is. April feels Jenna is being a phony. (We read Catcher in the Rye last year in English class. Sometimes April is like Holden Caulfield. Everybody is a "phony" in her eyes.) I think I respect Jenna for at least trying to be positive. There's something to be said for fake it until you make it.

For all that Jenna has lost her bossiness, grandma has doubled down on hers. She thinks we need saving and maybe we do. I never noticed conflict between her and Dad before but something is wrong between them now. I don't know what it is and I can hardly ask them about it. This is part of where I am struggling right now. I'm only twelve. The adults don't figure they have to let me in on the adult stuff. Jenna isn't all that observant. April notices things sometimes but she's so angry, it always affects how she sees them.

I could always talk to mom about stuff though. She never once told me I was too young to understand something. I missed her so much on the first day of school. I would have given anything to be able to pose for one of her dopey first day of school photos.

I've been reading bits of mom's journal. I want so much to binge read the entire thing but I make myself go one entry at a time. If they are on the longish side, I break them down and don't read them all at once.

I still haven't showed it to anybody else. It occurs to me to wonder if mom wanted one of us to find her journal and read it. I mean, why stash it in the laundry room? Why not put it in a closet? Or a drawer? Dad still hasn't cleaned out her clothes. Grandma was mad at him about it but he wouldn't budge. He said he wasn't ready. Grandma said he should just do it. Rip the Band-aid off, she told him. She said he would feel better but he wasn't having it. If mom had put the journal in her room, nobody would have even found it yet.

What she wrote was so sad, anxious and insecure. I have trouble reconciling the words she wrote with the mother I knew. If the entries weren't written in her distinctive straight up and down handwriting, I would have doubts that they were even written by her.

"We will not yet see truth nor beauty
Without seeing through the lens
Of our own perceptions
Everything colored by our experiences
And our expectations." - T.F. Forester

David
October
Three months after the accident

I don't know what Sarah was thinking. Honestly, since Allison died, I don't know what *anybody* is thinking. Everyone in my life seems overwhelmed and cranky or on the verge of a meltdown. I think everybody looks to me to hold it together. I know the girls do. But frankly, I feel like I might have a meltdown myself.

Sarah came over last night. Sarah was Allison's best friend, long before I met Allison, but we've still known each other for a long time. The company was welcome. We talked about Allison, of course. It was nice. I could talk to Sarah about Allison in a way I can't talk to the girls. Then I don't know what the hell happened. She hugged me. It was so nice to be touched.

In the months before Allison's accident, I felt like we had been struggling. She had stopped initiating sex. I'm not saying it was supposed to be all on her or anything. Obviously there should be give and take in a relationship. But Allison had always been very loving and physically affectionate. In the months before her accident, she stopped touching me.

She went along, if I initiated. She never complained and she participated in a perfunctory sort of way. But she didn't seem like she was into it. Her body was there but it felt like her brain was somewhere else. It wasn't just sex either. She was distant and distracted in all parts of our relationship for those last few months. I would catch glimpses of the old Allison. It was as if she had woken up from a daze and she would be herself again for a little while. Eventually, she would drift away again.

I wanted to talk to her about it. But it frightened me. So I kept putting off the conversation. Part of me really didn't want my questions answered. Part of me didn't want to know if we had a problem. I never did get to ask her. And now of course, I do know that we had a problem.

Last month that photography guy Alan or Adam or whatever the hell is name is, sat in my living room and told me they were having an affair. I don't understand why he wanted to tell me. Was he hoping for my approval? My blessing? My forgiveness? I can't even imagine what he was thinking in telling me. He claimed he loved her. Well good for him. His heart can be broken now too. Maybe that's petty or small of me but I don't have any generous and expansive gestures in me at the moment.

So last night, Sarah hugged me and I hugged her back. I don't even know who kissed who first. Things moved along quickly and predictably from there. I figured the inevitable was going to happen. Then she muttered something that made my heart stop along with every other activity. She said "I don't know how she could have cheated on you." I pushed her away from me and literally held her at arm's length. I asked her to repeat it. I'd heard it the first time really, but I needed it confirmed. I also needed to buy some time, to get myself under control.

At first, her pupils were still dilated. An aftermath of the plug pulled suddenly on desire. She said it again. "I don't know how she could have cheated on you." She said it louder the second time but with a lot less emotion and with growing bewilderment, then dismay. I could see the emotions change on her face as she realized what was happening.

"You knew," I accused her. "You were supposed to be my friend too."

This last was a little bit of a reach. We had never hung out without Allison despite having known one another for years. We both knew she was really Allison's friend. I also failed to tell her that Allison's infidelity was not news to me. But I wanted to lash out. I wanted to hurt her. Judging from the way her face collapsed, I did. She said she was sorry and started to cry. She reached for me and I moved away.

Part of me wanted nothing more than to hug her again and tell her it didn't matter. To lose myself in her warmth again. But I was so angry.

I was angry at Sarah, yes but even more angry at Allison. Allison was gone. I wasn't ever going to be able to express my anger to her again. But Sarah was here and she got the brunt of it. It wasn't really a betrayal on Sarah's part at all. It was all Allison.

"We may have before us
a veritable buffet of good choices
And yet, sometimes
We still make poor ones."
T.F. Forester

Allsion's Journal entry dated December 2012
Seventeen months before the accident

I feel bad about writing this in bed with David sleeping
peacefully right next to me. I have often written in my journal, in
bed, but writing about this, with him so close, feels wrong
somehow. And isn't that just like me, to overreact about the
writing when the thing I'm writing about is actually the problem
and not the writing itself really. I'm so obtuse sometimes in these
journal entries. It's as if I don't even want to tell myself the truth.
But the truth is Adam kissed me tonight. The truth is I kissed him
back. I should have stopped him. I should have walked away. I
should have reminded him (and myself) that I'm married. But I
didn't. I don't know what's wrong with me. Why can't I just
behave like a normal person? I'm not going to see Adam anymore.
I'm going to let the fellowship go. It felt wonderful to be chosen
and I really did want to learn more about photography. But I
can't. Because I can't be sure that I can be with Adam and not let
him kiss me again. And not kiss him back. And not kiss him in
the first place. And it's a slippery slope because even though I
stopped that kiss and said "I can't" and pushed him gently away,
my body wanted a whole lot more than that kiss. I'm not sure I
deserved the fellowship anyway.

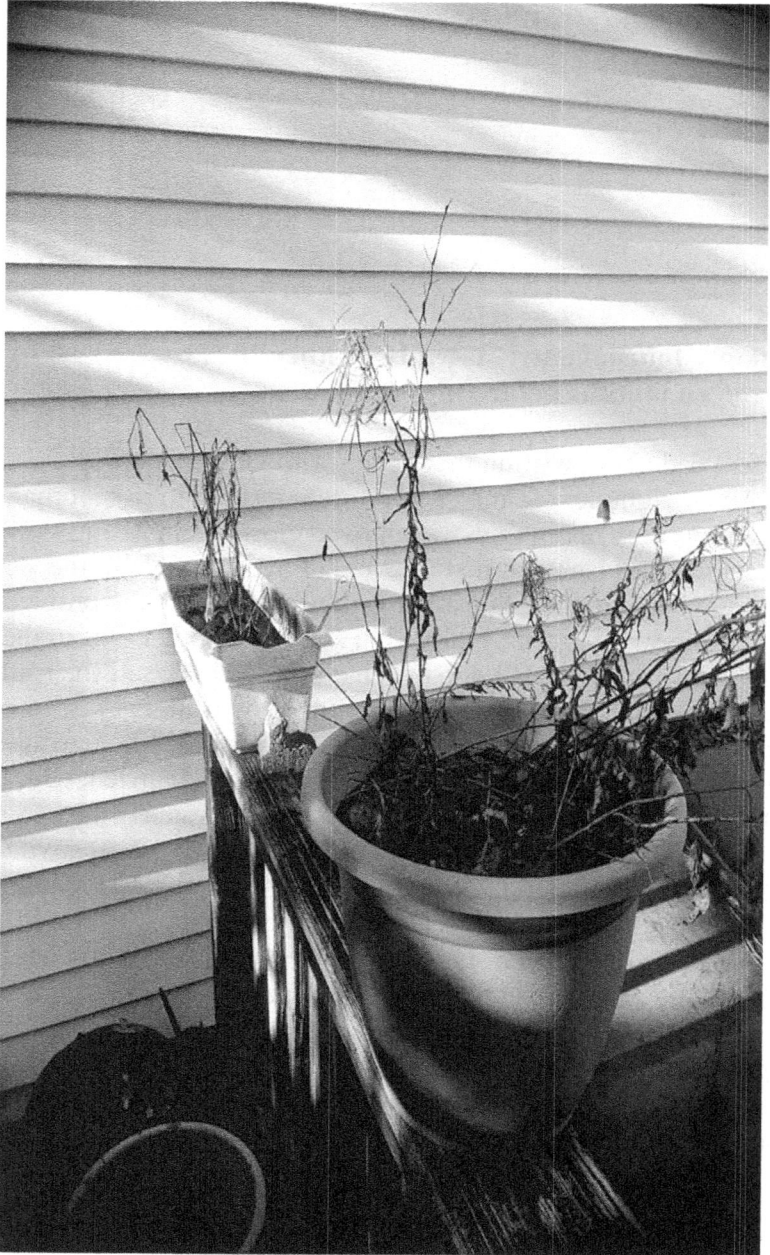

From Allison's Photography Show, September 2013

*"Some hearts feel so deeply
It seems like it would be better
To feel nothing at all."*
T.F. Forester

April
October
Three months after the accident

    I hate school. I'm not dumb. I can do the work. I just don't see the point. I'm only a sophomore this year but they're already pushing college. I might go. I might not. But I'm certainly not going to go just because the guidance department thinks it's a good idea or because my school wants to parade around all those numbers of how many kids went to college.

    I sleep over at Elise's every weekend now. I can tell that Dad would like me to be home more often and I feel a little bit bad, but I hate being home. I can't do it. The first weekend after school started, Elise dragged me into her room and shut the door. She held a finger to her lips and admonished me to be quiet even though I hadn't even said anything yet. She hauled a paper bag out from under her bed. The bag contained a six-pack of beer. Kids at school talked about drinking all of the time but honestly, I had never tried it. Elise claimed she'd been drunk at camp the summer before but I wasn't so sure about that. Elise embellished her stories sometimes. I wouldn't call her a liar but she totally stretched the truth if it suited her purposes.

    We each drank three of the beers. It didn't taste good but Elise kept drinking, so I kept drinking. We drank them fast. Afterward, I felt light and silly and not sad at all. I wasn't scared of things. Normally, everything is scary for me. Going to school is scary. Being at home is scary. Losing my mom is so scary that I go way out of my way to not think about that one at all. Anything and everything can trigger my anxiety and I hate it. I don't tell people that. Elise doesn't know and I don't think my sisters do either. If Dad knows, it's because mom told him. Mom understood it but Mom is gone.

I was going to talk to mom about it over the summer. I was even going to ask her maybe to take me to a doctor and see if I could get some medication or something. Some days, I'm so scared, I don't even want to be around anymore. I don't think I was going to tell her that. Now I don't think I'll tell anybody anything. There isn't anybody who can help me and I'm not going to ask. Screw it. I'll figure it out on my own or not. Who cares?

I know one thing; that little buzzy, lightheaded, "I have no worries" feeling wore off way too soon. When it did, I *really* wished I had three more beers.

From Allison's Photography Show September 2013

"The stories we tell ourselves about the past
are just that – stories
Sure, there are truths in them
But memories, like hearts
Can be fickle."
T.F. Forester

Jenna
October
Three months after the accident

I'm obsessed with a couple of things right now, aside from
being pregnant and wondering how that it going to change the
entire rest of my life and missing my mom. Those things
honestly take up a lot of my emotional bandwidth but
occasionally I can step back a bit and obsess over something else.

The first something else is a black and white photo Mom took
of an empty rowboat. I don't think Dad would have thought of it,
but I went down to the gallery where she had been showing her
photos. I talked to that Adam guy who had been her photography
teacher or whatever he was. I asked him for all of Mom's photos.
He gave me everything she had been exhibiting as well as a whole
folder of other stuff which hadn't been framed or edited or
whatever. The rowboat photo was in this other folder. I had
never seen this photo before.

I don't know where the picture was taken. When we were little
and Mom just took a lot of pictures for fun, she used to haul us
with her. She'd say, "Well, okay, today, we're going to take
pictures of trains or waterfalls or rock formations or whatever she
was interested in. She's pack us all into the car with snacks and
off we'd go. Dad was usually at work but she'd make day trips
out of it. She tried to make it fun for us too.

Later on, after she won the photography fellowship, she often
went off on her own. We had all gotten older and weren't all that
interested in going any more. I think Charlotte still went with her
a few times by herself. I felt like I was too busy to go, when I
was in high school. April thought she was too cool to go or
whatever. I wish I'd made the time though. I can't imagine what
April thinks. She wasn't very nice to Mom, the last couple of
years. She wasn't very nice to *anyone.*

Anyway, this black and white photo shows a rowboat, just sitting half in and half out of the water. All I can think of is Charon the Ferryman, waiting to take passengers to Hades. The image is from Greek mythology. There are no people in Mom's rowboat photo, mind you. But I can imagine the ferryman in that little boat. Dour-faced and serious, waiting to take each passenger's coin for their final trip.

I can't shake this image out of my head. I don't have any idea *when* she took this picture. I assume it was in the last couple of years after she won the fellowship and after we stopped going on those trips with her. But I don't know and it drives me crazy because it almost feels like she knew something terrible was going to happen.

This makes absolutely no sense. There is nothing bad about the picture. It just makes me *feel* bad. Unsettled. Almost guilty. She couldn't have known that something bad was going to happen to her. And it's just a photo of a boat. I don't understand why it freaks me out but I can't stop looking at this photo.

Maybe my reaction is just a sign that Mom was a great photographer although she would have been all modest about it. But isn't that what good art is supposed to do? Isn't it supposed to touch you in some way? To unsettle you? To evoke strong emotions? Instead of consoling me, this thought just makes me more sad about the whole thing.

The other thing that gets me is a memory. A couple of times, when I was really little, mom and I went camping with grandma. Dad stayed home with April, who was a baby. Mom wasn't crazy about camping but Grandma wanted to go. Mom always had the ability to make the best of something. I so admired this about her.

I feel like I spend all of my time wishing for things to be different, especially lately. Mom said it was okay to try to improve things and okay to have hope about the future. But she said you also had to embrace things as they were, right now, even if those things didn't seem that good to you. She said you couldn't change things without being able to accept them first.

She said what we resist, persists. I never really understood any of this. I'm not sure I even do now although I might be beginning to. Maybe.

At any rate, we only ended up going camping a couple of times. Maybe Grandma felt bad about making Mom go when she didn't really love it. Maybe it wasn't as much fun as she thought it would be. I don't know. I was really little and I never thought to ask when I was older. In fact, I hadn't thought about those trips at all, in years.

Anyway, one night, on one of those trips, I woke Mom up, because I had to pee. She groggily walked me to the bathroom, holding my hand. Grandma stayed asleep. On the way back, Mom pointed out the stars to me. She told me that at home, we had something called light pollution, which made the stars difficult to see, but out in the woods, where the campground was, there wasn't a lot of man made light and you could see them better. As we were admiring the night sky, we heard a terrible noise. It sounded like a baby crying. I couldn't understand why a baby would be crying in the woods at night.

Mom said it wasn't a baby at all but an animal called a fisher cat. I thought I saw green glowing eyes over by the treeline. I started to cry. I was so scared. Mom gently led me back to the tent and rubbed my back until I fell asleep. I woke up a bunch of times during the night and every time I did, mom was right there, wide awake, with a smile or a reassuring touch.

It occurs to me now that she probably stayed up all night, watching me sleep but not sleeping herself. When I read about fisher cats in school later the next year, I was scared all over again. But Mom never seemed scared. She was calm. She made me feel calm. She did that with all of us, whenever we were scared. She always made us think we could be brave. She always made us feel like we could do whatever we needed to do. I think she was fearless. I wish I could be fearless.

From Allison's "Things Fall Apart" Playlist
   21) Off To The Races-Lana del Rey
   22) Breathe Me-Sia
   23) I Am Still Here-Damien Jurado
   24) Heartbreak Hotel- Elvis
   25) Can't Find My Way Home-Blind Faith

"I want only to fix things for you
Yet some things are not fixable
And some cannot be fixed by me."
T.F. Forester

Cindy
October
Three months after the accident

I don't even know what to do with those girls. David needs to step in and be a better parent. Jenna is getting as stubborn as her mom was. I can tell she misses school and none of her friends seem to be around anymore. I'm not sure if it's their choice or Jenna's. Maybe they don't feel they have anything in common with her now that she's pregnant.

I think it's more likely that Jenna is just isolating herself. There's no sign of the baby's father. I asked Jenna what had happened there. She said she didn't want to talk about it. I want to get mad at her about it. But I've tried to restrain myself. I understand that I might be projecting a little bit. I understand that some of it might be my issue. Maybe even more than some of it.

Allison's dad and I got divorced when she was a toddler. He was in and out of her life until she was ten. Finally, I told him, "Look, this girl does not need a sometime father. She doesn't need you to show up and get her hopes up, then disappear and break her heart over and over again. What happened between you and I, is irrelevant. But as far as Allison is concerned, you need to be in or out. Make a choice. Commit," I told him.

He chose out. I didn't like his choice but I had issued the ultimatum and he took it. I did the best I could as a single mom to make sure life stable. So who am I to push Jenna on the single motherhood issue? It's not such a big deal these days anyway, although it's still a hard thing to manage even if society no longer looks down on your for it.

But I do think Jenna is withdrawing and it isn't good for her. I want her to have a baby shower. I want her to find out the baby's sex and have one of those gender reveal parties. Jenna says she isn't going to find out. "What does it matter?" she asks. "A baby is a baby. You don't get to chose whether you have a boy or a girl and I don't care either way."

This worries me somewhat. I understand that the circumstances aren't ideal but I would like for her to be more excited about this. It seems like she isn't invested in the pregnancy. Oh, she takes her prenatal vitamins. She's walking every day. She seems to be eating well. She goes dutifully to her appointments but she doesn't seem to care all that much. Initially, she seemed more happy about it or at least she was pretending to be happy. Now it seems like just getting through her day is a struggle for her.

I badgered her about the baby shower and she promised to at least think about it although I sense she's just brushing me off. Agreeing to consider it but hoping to avoid it if it actually comes right down to it.

April is another matter. She's angry. She's angry with Jenna for being pregnant in the first place. She's angry with Charlotte for being young. She's angry with me and with her dad, although I don't know why. I suspect she's angry with Allison for dying. That one worries me. I can handle her being angry with me for whatever reason. But she's never going to be able to tell Allison how she feels. She's going to have to resolve those feelings without Allison's input and I don't know that she will be able to.

I don't always know what Charlotte thinks. It isn't that she's uncommunicative. She talks to me. She talks to her dad and also her sisters. Yet every time we have a conversation, I have the sense of things unsaid. I can't even imagine what those things might be. In a way, Charlotte reminds me of her mom the most. Still waters run deep. Allison always seemed like a person who put everything out there.

Yet now, we are learning that she had secrets. Her drinking had become problematic and nobody saw it. I suspected, of course. I listened to some mother's instinct about that. But I, like the rest of her family had never *seen* it. I can't help but wonder what other secrets she may have been keeping.

"Would that I could seek respite
From the weight of my mistakes
I am willing to own them
But would just put them down for a bit
For they are heavy."
T.F. Forester

Sarah
October
Three months after the accident

Now, I've managed to ruin everything. I didn't intend to kiss David. It just sort of happened. Yes, I had a thing for him but for a few moments there, it just felt like we were both grieving for Allison. It seemed like our physical proximity could help heal our mutual grief.

Then I blew it. I shouldn't have told him that I knew about the affair. Or maybe I should have told him much sooner than I did. I don't even know. I'm not sure I see any way where it ends well. I had to keep Allison's secrets. I hated to but I had to. He doesn't understand and he didn't let me explain it to him. That was four days ago but it feels like a torturous four years.

I want to call him. I want to go over there and talk to him. I want us to both go back to being sad about losing Allison, but together. We could commiserate. We could talk. I wouldn't even touch him again, if he didn't want me to. Or I would if he did want me to. Whatever he wanted would be okay with me.

I can't process this loss by myself and I don't have anybody else. Allison was my best friend for so long. How can I cope with not having her to talk to? She would have had the right words to help me deal with this. Maybe part of me just wanted to be close to David the other day, so I could feel close to Allison.

I've begun talking to her in my head. That sounds crazy, I know. What kind of person talks to their dead best friend? She knew how to handle things. She knew what to do when everything fell apart. Me, I don't feel like I know how to a handle anything. At least Allison isn't talking back to me yet in the conversations in my head. For now, they are simultaneously blissfully and depressingly one-sided.

From Allison's Photography Show September 2013

*"Pull me down oh pull me down
To that place where nothing hurts."*
T.F. Forester

April
Late October
One hundred and twenty-three days after the accident

Elise talked her cousin into buying us vodka. It was so much stronger than beer. It worked faster too. I love that feeling. I suppose it's being drunk. But when you learn about being drunk in health class or whatever, it makes it seem like drunk equals out of control. For me it feels like more control than I've ever had. I don't feel worried or anxious. I'm not thinking about school or Jenna's baby or mom and the photography teacher or whatever. Nothing hurts. Nothing is terrifying. It's the pain and the fear that feels out of control for me and they have felt out of control for most of my life. When I drink, everything feels calm and okay. I have more control, not less.

From Allison's "Things Fall Apart" Playlist
26)Tomorrow Wendy-Concrete Blonde
27)Sorrow-The National
28)Violet-Hole
29)End of the Innocence-Don Henley
30)Heart Shaped Box-Nirvana

"Sad and sorry
So very, very sorry
Yet feeling powerless
As I lay down on the tracks
Before the speeding train
of my bad decisions."
T.F. Forester

Allison's Journal entry dated March 2014
Four months before the accident

I never thought I'd be that wife who had an affair. Didn't affairs happen when you no longer loved your spouse? I love David. I have always loved him and I don't see myself *not* loving him anytime soon. Although, if he knew what I was about, he might chose to no longer love me. I can't say that I'd blame him if he did. It would break my heart. But I would understand if he didn't want to love me anymore. I don't know if I love Adam or not. I am a different person with him than I am at home with David and the girls.

That woman is a lot more bad ass than I am. She doesn't struggle, She has no guilt. She does whatever she wants to do. I'm not sure we should show different versions of ourselves to different people. I get that there are levels of knowing people. Most of us aren't going to share our most intimate secrets with acquaintances from our kids' schools or other people we barely know. But Adam and I have been pretty intimate. It seems like he and David should see the same Allison and I know that they don't.

It's not accidental. It's by design. It strikes me as manipulative and I have never seen myself that way before. It makes me sad but not sad enough to put a stop to the behavior. I have too much inertia. I can neither end the affair nor be my full authentic self with either them. Yet this issue of authenticity is an odd one. Because both David and Adam see parts of me that are true. It's just that neither is the whole truth. The whole truth is to scary to contemplate. Were I to show either of them the whole me, light and dark together, neither one of them would want me.

I have never really wanted to own all the complicated parts of myself. I've embraced the good girl, good wife, good mother and good daughter roles. They seem safe enough. But I've always tried to ignore the darker, shadowy sides of myself. Those sides are lost and anxious and sometimes angry and they frighten me. I don't want anyone to see those.

From Allison's "Things Fall Apart" Playlist
31) Don't Dream It's Over-Crowded House
32) Don't Speak-No Doubt
33) Disarm-Smashing Pumpkins
34) Wicked Game-Chris Issak
35) Cut Your Bangs-Girlpool

"And what is 'normal' anyway?
How can we aspire to a state
Which is merely illusory?"
T.F. Forester

Charlotte
November
Four months since the accident

I volunteered to help Grandma make Thanksgiving dinner at our house. I don't really love cooking. I never really helped all that much when mom made Thanksgiving dinner. But I so crave normalcy. Right after Mom died, the guidance counselor at school told me that things would seem more normal as time went by. I don't know how much time she had in mind, but things seems to get more difficult on a daily basis.

It's almost like Mom was the glue that held us all together, and without her, we fall apart. Even though we are family and even though we love each other, it feels like we can't make anything work without mom. I don't know if this is just how we feel or if Mom really did a lot of behind the scenes work, keeping us together.

Regardless, I have it in my head that if we could just have a nice normal Thanksgiving, that maybe we could be okay again. I don't really know how it will seem "normal" without Mom but I feel like we need to try. Suddenly, I care about tablecloths and napkins and china. These are things I have never cared about before. But I think if I could make it perfect, we might be okay. Some part of me rationalizes that this is ridiculous. A nice holiday changes nothing. It doesn't matter.

I cling to this. I obsess over this. I'm sorry I ever found Mom's journal. She started to talk about kissing her photography teacher and I couldn't read any more. I hid it away. Every day, I think I will read more and every day, I can't seem to make myself pick it up again. I read things about my mother in her own words that I never would have suspected from her. But I know they are true because she wrote them.

What if other things I've never suspected are also true? What if she never actually loved us? I could find that sort of things out if I kept reading, maybe. Who knows? But that's the sort of thing I can't know. I don't want to know.

Then I think, "but what if reading helps me to understand what happened? What if her journal helps me sort it all out in my own head?" But I can't. I'm afraid. I go round and round.

No. Thanksgiving. Gratitude and Great Grandma Mildred's fine china. Normal. Just like always. We'll pretend that mom is on a vacation or a photography expedition or she got a new job which made her travel. Anything at all but she is gone and she kept secrets from us.

From Allison's Photography Show September 2013

"We see the things we want to-
The things which are easy.
We look away
From that which shakes us to our core."
T.F. Forester

David
November
Four months since the accident

I used to feel like I got things right some of the time. I've been reasonably successful in my career. I have three beautiful daughters and up until a few months ago, I was happily married to the love of my life. At least I thought I was. Turns out, maybe she wasn't as happy as I was. It turns out maybe she was not as happy as I thought she was and that hurts even more. Not seeing that, is just one of the many things on my list of stuff I'm not getting right anymore. Maybe any sense of rightness was an illusion anyway.

My mother-in-law, who was never overbearing or annoying when Allison was alive, is in my face all of the time now. She's telling me what I should do about this or that but mostly what I should do about the girls. Some of her advice is even good but I resent it anyway. She acts like I have no idea what I'm doing. Honestly, that's probably way too close to the truth for my comfort. This is why it really, really irritates me.

I don't know what to do with a pregnant daughter who sees her dreams slipping away. I don't know what to do with an angry distant fifteen-year-old who wants to spend all of her time locked in her room or at the neighbor's house. I don't know what to do with a twelve-year-old who seems wise beyond not only her years but beyond anyone's years.

And those aren't the only places where I feel like I'm failing. I am sorry I pushed Sarah away. But I'm not sure I can fix that and if I do, is it only for my own selfish purposes? I'm lonely, dammit. Yet I also feel a certain sense of betrayal. Still, if I'm being honest here, and I suppose I am, that betrayal is on Allison. But is it fair to try to reconnect with Sarah just because I'm sad and confused? Because I miss my wife? That seems pretty unfair to Sarah. I think I over reacted. I'm pretty sure I owe her an apology. After all, Sarah must be grieving too. I'm not sure I can get out of my own way enough to implement a reconciliation.

It's all a mess. Everything. All of it. I read something once, which said that women often do better in divorce scenarios because women are better connected with one another. Often, for men, their primary support person is their wife. Sure, I have guy friends but we don't really talk about stuff like that. My friends talk about sports and sex. If it doesn't involve balls of some sort, they're out.

Allison cheated on me. She kept secrets from me and she didn't seem fully invested in our marriage for those last few months although she never even hinted at wanting a divorce. Why did she stop communicating with me? Was it because of the affair or did the affair happen because I wasn't fulfilling her needs in some way? I'm not so arrogant as to believe that whatever went wrong between us was all her fault, affair or not. I am confused and sad and angry. Mostly angry. Isn't anger one of the stages of grief? Somebody wrote a whole book about that, I think.

Yet, as angry as I am with her about everything, I would give anything to talk to her right now. To ask her advice. To hear her tell me I'm being foolish or that I'm overreacting. To hear her laugh. I would even listen to her telling me she didn't love me anymore because at least, for a few moments, I would be in her presence and I would hear her voice. I would give anything.

"Everything changes
You can have goals and dreams
You may even achieve them
But the straight path you envisioned
Does not exist
It twists back upon itself
And turns with lurching abruptness
It is imperfect and impermanent."
T.F. Forester

Jenna
November
Four months since the accident

I like to think I was doing pretty well over the summer and early fall. I missed going back to school, of course. I also miss my mom like crazy. But I didn't feel like I was falling apart. I saw friends over Thanksgiving break. Dad and Grandma both seemed incredibly relieved that I hung out with people. It was an unmitigated disaster but I didn't tell them that. I pretended to be cheerful and happy. This is what I do.

April gives me crap about it all the time. She claims I'm being inauthentic. What she doesn't understand, what *no one* seems to understand, is that I cannot allow myself to be sad. If I allow that sadness to take over, I will never not be sad again. It will destroy me. I will be the first person to actually turn to dust from the intensity of their sadness. That sounds overly dramatic, I know. And no, I know that I won't actually turn to dust. But I won't recover either. The pregnancy. Jason's abandonment. The loss of my mother. These things are all too much. If I allow myself to actually feel the weight of these things, it will destroy me.

When I saw my friends from school over break, they wanted to drink. I couldn't because of the baby, of course but even if I hadn't been pregnant, I'm not sure I ever want anything to do with alcohol again. Mom had a problem and we didn't even know. Except that I had suspicions and I didn't act on them. So some of what happened could be my fault.

Then, my friends talked about school and I missed it terribly. I also heard that Jason had actually gone back to college despite insisting that he wasn't. I heard he'd had a string of girlfriends and partied all the time. So he didn't care about me. He had *never* cared about me. One friend suggested that Jason really did care about me and the baby, he just didn't know how to show it. I know she was just trying to make me feel better but it definitely did not.

Sometimes, Mom and Dad used to argue about books. They were both big readers and they could have these crazy, passionate discussions about fictional characters and their motives. I can remember them talking about love and the "Scarlet Letter" by Nathaniel Hawthorne. Dad said Reverend Dimmesdale really loved Hester and baby Pearl but he was a product of his times and was too constrained by his Puritan ideals to do the right thing by them.

No, Mom, insisted. That wasn't love. If he really loved them, he would have manned up, taken care if them and truly loved them, openly. I read the book, years after I overheard the conversation. I think I agree with Mom on this one. If you love someone but can't or won't show them, you may as well not love them at all.

So hanging out with my friends was truly awful. But I smiled. I laughed. When Dad and Grandma grilled me about it, I shared some funny pieces of the conversations we'd had. I promised I would see them all again over winter break. I acted happy. I acted like I didn't care what Jason did. No one knew I was completely bereft. Nobody needs to see my broken heart.

"I don't want to hear your insights
Even if they are true
Especially if they are true
There are things I am too willful
To look at right now."
T.F. Forester

April
November
Four months after the accident

Elsie and I had a giant fight. I don't know if it's fixable. I don't even know if I want to fix it. I have been spending every weekend at her house since school started. We've been drinking quite a bit lately. It's been fun. At least I thought it was. Last weekend, Elise told me she thought we should drink less. She gave me some bullshit line about wanting to try harder at school. Seriously? Who cares about school? She said she thought we were overdoing. She said she was worried we might have a problem. I got really angry. "You mean you think *I* have a problem?" I demanded.

"I think you might," she said softly.

I got even angrier, which was a a scary thing, and stormed out. Who was she to be judging me anyway? She was the person who first thought we should try that beer. What was wrong with her? I didn't have a problem.

A tiny voice at the back of my head tried protesting. It tried to say that Elise was the only real friend I had. It quietly asked if Elise could be right. Was it possible that I did have a problem? Thank God, that voice was small. It was easy to drown it out. That voice was panicky. I don't need to listen to panic crap. I'll have to find a new connection for alcohol but I can do that. I'm not ever going back to feeling anxious and sad all the time. I can't. It will be the end of me.

From Allison's "Things Fall Apart" Playlist
36)Long Ride Home-Patty Griffin
37)Eve Of Destruction-Barry Maguire
38)It Must Have Been Love-Roxette
39)Safe and Sound-Sheryl Crow
40)River-Joni Mitchell

"I will look back
On every word you wrote
Re-reading them both literally
And searching for nuance
I will hold those words
Close to my heart
As if they were sacred
For they are
And all that I have left"
T.F. Forester

David
December
Five months after the accident

Cindy has been after me to clean out some of Allison's things. She claims it will be therapeutic for me. I know she probably has my best interests at heart but she's a pain in the ass sometimes. Until a few years ago, Jenna had her own room and April and Charlotte shared a room. When Jenna went to college last year, April moved into Jenna's old room and was thrilled to have her own space. But Jenna's baby is due in February. April is going to have to go back to sharing with Charlotte.

There was bitter complaining on April's part, but it is what it is. I'm going to move into Jenna's old room and give Jenna the master bedroom for her and the baby. It's not ideal for anyone but I don't need a lot of space for just me. I don't sleep anymore anyway, so what does it matter where I do (or don't as is the case) do it? Sting sang "The Bed's Too Big Without You" and that's how I feel every single night. Allison is missing everywhere from my life, but nowhere so much, as at night, in bed. So, by logistical necessity more than anything I'm starting to go through some of Allison's things.

It's surprisingly easy to let go of clothes and shoes. There are a few things she wore all of the time which give me pause- a worn Beatles tee-shirt. The red dress she wore on a Valentine's Day date a few years ago. The sweater I bought her last Christmas. But lots of things, I'd never seen her wear. Or maybe I just wasn't paying attention.

This whole theme of not paying enough attention runs through my brain almost constantly these days. I should have seen that Allison was in trouble. I should have seen that *we* were in trouble. What was so important that I was oblivious? Did I purposefully not see things? Could I have fixed or changed anything if I had been paying attention? I go round and round with this. I accomplish nothing but just can't seem to let it go.

Under a pair of winter boots, I find an orange Nike shoe box. It has "Just Do It" emblazoned across the cover. At first, I'm just going to dismiss it as sneakers but the heft of it is wrong for shoes, somehow. A little voice at the back of my head insists that I know what's in this box. It advises that like Pandora, I should under no circumstances, open this box. It warns, that I will be sad and hurt and God even knows what other emotions will surface, if I open it. I ignore the voice and lift the lid.

It's still amazing to me, how so much about Allison strikes me in a visceral, punch in the gut, take my breath away kind of way. This is no exception. I sit there, on the floor of the closet, reminding myself to breathe. I sit there for what feels like a really long time.

The box is full of cassette tapes. We haven't owned a cassette player in years, yet Allison has kept these tapes. Was it by accident? Was it by design? Did she forget what was in the box or did she lovingly keep it on purpose? I'm so flustered that I will never know the answer to this question. I focus on breathing some more.

On the inside of the lid, Allison has drawn a smiley face, a peace symbol and a heart. In Sharpie marker, she's written "Love Is Mix Tapes".

Love is mix tapes. After our first meeting at the tutoring center in college, Allison and I traded phone numbers. I was supposed to help her with algebra after all. I called her about a week after we first met. I knew she'd had a big exam and ostensibly, I was calling to see how it had gone. The truth was I wanted to call her ten minutes after she left the tutoring center just to hear her voice again. The truth was, waiting a whole week was torture.

It took several rings for her to pick up but she sounded genuinely happy to talk to me. This was before everyone had cell phones. I called the landline in her dorm. This life without instant connectivity is so foreign to my girls. They can't even imagine that world. It feels like the stone age or something to them.

Anyway, Allison said she and her roommate where making blueberry muffins in her roommate's toaster oven. She said it like we were old friends and not like I was just some guy who was trying to help her with algebra.

"How did the exam go?" I finally manged to ask.

"I dunno," she said and her voice was so expressive, I swear, I could hear her shrug over the phone line. "That thing you explained about integers was helpful, I think, but I'm definitely going to need more help. I'm such a math moron."

"You're not a moron," I said dumbly.

"Well, you know..." she replied and chuckled.

I wanted to yell, "No, I don't know, but please tell me. Take as long as you want. Filibuster. Explain in ridiculous detail. Just please, keep talking to me."

I didn't say anything though and a few seconds of painful silence stretched out over the phone line. Just when I was sure she was going to thank me for calling and hang up on me, she asked "Do you have class tomorrow afternoon? Would you like to go to the cafe in the student union for ice cream?"

I only had morning classes the next day but I would have skipped *anything* in order to see her again. I didn't tell her that though.

Instead, I said something stupid.

I said, "Are you sure you want to go for ice cream? It's kind of cold out. Wouldn't you rather go for coffee or something?"

As soon as the words were out of my mouth, I was mentally kicking myself. Unsmooth, dude. Go wherever the hell she wants to go. She wants to go with *you*. So just go with it.

She was unfazed.

"No, I've really been craving a hot fudge sundae. I don't think coffee's going to do it for me when what I really need is chocolate."

She laughed again. Her laugh seemed to come so easily. It made me feel like maybe the world had been filled with humor for years but I'd never had the ability to see it. I not only wanted to hear her laugh again, I vowed that soon, I would be the one to make her laugh.

So, we went for ice cream despite the fact that it was November and 35 degrees out.

"Do you like music?" she'd asked me on that first date.

I told her I did. We had a huge, rambling discussion about music. I'd always considered my musical tastes to be fairly well-rounded but Allison had more wildly eclectic tastes than anyone I'd ever met. She knew about bands I'd never even heard of. She could talk about big band music just as easily as she could heavy metal or alternative. And she was passionate about it. I would later learn that if Allison loved something or someone, she loved all the way with no reservations. Go big or go home, she always said. Nothing compared to the way she shone when she was excited about something.

Despite my reaction to her when we first met in the tutoring center, I might have had a chance at not loving her had I never seen her again. Maybe. But after spending three hours eating ice cream and talking about music with her, I was a lost cause. I was doomed in the best possible way.

It occurs to me now, that we just recently passed the anniversary of that first date. Allison almost always marked it in some way, even if it was just with a hug and saying "Do you remember?" I don't remember her remembering last year. Just one more clue that things were wrong. Just one more clue that I missed.

We met for ice cream again the next week. When she saw me, she gave me a huge hug and handed me a cassette tape.

"I like to make music mixes for people," she said almost shyly. It was the first time I'd seen her act a little insecure. It was almost like she thought I might reject her gift. There was not a chance of that but it was still hopelessly endearing.

"I love to introduce people to music they might not have heard before," she continued. "Might be a little bit of an odd mix though. Hope you like it."

I assured her that I would.

Odd mix was a bit of an understatement. Her mixes bounced all over the place just like Allison herself. They were crazy and fabulous. That tape was the first of many she would make me. I listened to every single song on every single tape. Later she made a few on CDs too.

She made them for me for years. For anniversaries and birthdays and business trips and just because. She made one when the girls were little and called it "Middle of the Night Music". She said sometimes she was just so exhausted, she could barely even remember her own name, no less song lyrics. But she loved to sing to them and made a tape of songs she loved and pretty much knew by heart and just sand along.

Somewhere after Charlotte was born, she stopped making them. We still listened to music together in the car sometimes. She would still occasionally say, "I just discovered this new song, I love" and play it for me. But there were no more mix tapes. I get it. We had three young kids and she'd gone back to work part time doing marketing for non-profits. The truth was I didn't even realize that she'd stopped making them or even missed them all that much at the time.

I missed them now though. Those tapes were almost like an insight into her soul. I didn't realize I'd moved away from having such insight in the last few years. Maybe I would have to trawl EBAY for a cassette player. Or maybe I should just leave well enough alone. I traced the letters of "Love Is Mix Tapes" with my finger, closed the lid and sat there for a very long time.

Allison's first mix tape to David circa 1991

Side one:
I Can't wait - Nu Shooz
Don't Go Breakin' My Heart - Elton John & Kiki Dee
Superman's Song - Crash Test Dummies
Just Like Heaven - The Cure
Promises in the Dark - Pat Benetar
Money Changes Everything - Cyndi Lauper
Julie Don't Live Here Anymore - ELO

Side two:
Bloody Well Right - Supertramp
Love Don't Live Here Anymore - Madonna
In a Big Country - Big Country
Tales of Brave Ulysses - Cream
Your Wildest Dreams - Moody Blues
Scenes From An Italian Restaurant - Billy Joel
Tom's Diner - Suzanne Vega

"Sing to me
Songs of love and pain and frustration and
hopelessness
Find songs
Which express the things that you cannot."
T.F. Forester

Jenna
December
Five months after the accident

Dad has been going through mom's stuff. I offered to help and so did Charlotte but he told us it was something he needed to do by himself. I guess I get that. He dug up a box of tapes that Mom had made him when they were in college. I don't think we even own a tape player anymore. He gave me two home made CDs though. We do still have a CD player, although I don't actually own any CDs and I don't think my sisters do either.

No songs were listed on the CDs or the envelopes they were in. They were simply labeled "Middle of the Night Music" and "Middle of the Night Music vol.2" in Mom's handwriting. There was a little smiley face on on of them. Dad said it was music mom had played for us when we were little. I sort of remembered but not really. It was like one of those things you can only see peripherally. When you look at it head on, it disappears. Sometimes memory is like that. You can't focus too hard on retrieving it. You just have to let it come to you.

I had almost thought they would be some kind of kid's music but no, it was a whole weird mom mix of regular music. Mom liked all kinds of music. She always sang to us and played music in the car on our trips. She liked a little bit of everything, I think.

I started to play the first CD. The first couple of songs were ones I'd heard before but they didn't seem to have any particular meaning or memories associated with them. The third song was "Can't Take My Eyes Off You." It's an old song. I don't know who does it. I suppose I could Google it but I didn't. It doesn't matter who sang it anyway. When it came on, I had a very clear memory of April and Charlotte and I, in our PJs on a snow day. Mom was signing along and the music was loud. We were all dancing around and laughing. There wasn't anything special about the memory and yet everything about it was special all at the same time. It hit me like a truck. I had to turn the CD off.

Middle of the Night Music
1) Slip Sliding Away - Paul Simon
2) American Pie - Don McLean
3) Can't Take My Eyes Of You - Frankie Valli and the Four Seasons
4) Love, Me - Colin Ray
5) The Last Resort - The Eagles
6) I Love - Tom T Hall
7) I Need You - America
8) The Man Who Shot Liberty Valance - Gene Pitney
9) Waterloo Sunset - The Kinks

Middle of the Night Music Vol. 2
1) Time After Time - Cyndi Lauper
2) A Month of Sundays - Don Henley
3) Too Much Love Will Kill You - Queen
4) Gentleman Who Fell - Milla Jovovich
5) Maybe-from Annie
6) Always - Bon Jovi
7) Telephone Line - ELO
8) You Don't Know Me - Jann Arden
9) Bell Bottom Blues - Derek and the Dominos

That was a few days ago and I haven't played it since although it's still sitting in the CD player in the living room with vol. 2 still sitting on top of the CD player. It got me thinking though. A few years ago, I set up an online music streaming service for mom. There was some low introductory price and I thought she might like it because she liked music so much. I gave it to her for her birthday. In retrospect, it seems kind of lame. I mean, it was something she could have easily set up for herself had she wanted to. But she had seemed pleased with it nonetheless. She had said it was something she never would have thought to do on her own. I don't know if that was true or not.

I didn't know if mom had continued to pay the subscription fee or if she had simply let it lapse when her promotional year was up. When they pulled her car out of the pond, they did find her phone but it was so water damaged, we couldn't get it to turn on. But the streaming service let you use multiple devices. I logged onto our family desktop. This was the one we'd all done homework on in the living room. I pulled up the streaming service and entered the password I'd set it up with.

It turned out mom hadn't changed the password and had continued to pay the subscription fee. She had added a lot of music in the last few years too. This particular streaming service showed how often you'd played certain songs and certain playlists. There was one playlist that caught my attention. It was named "Things Fall Apart; The Center Cannot Hold" and it had been played 143 times from January to July. The last playing was July 1, the day mom died.

I tend to name my playlists things like "Relaxation" or "Gym Mix" and so do most people I know. Not mom though. I opened the internet and looked up "Things fall apart, the center cannot hold." It turned out to be from a poem by W.B. Yeats about the first world war. I was pretty sure Mom didn't have any interest in the first world war and the songs were all contemporary. It was a beautiful sort of haunting quote but what did she think was falling apart and why had she played these songs so much?

I didn't know a lot of the songs on the playlist but suddenly I felt like I needed to hear them. All of them. All of the sudden, I wanted, no, *needed* to hear every note and every lyric. There were almost sixty songs on the playlist. Mom must have been listening to a lot of music in her car on her photography expeditions or whatever. I hadn't really noticed her playing very much music at home.

It took almost four hours to listen to this playlist. The songs were sad or angry or sometimes both at once. In addition to "Can't Take My Eyes Off You" I could also remember her singing "Build Me Up Buttercup" and the Beatles' "Eight Days a Week". None of these songs were fun or fluffy though.

Individually, they might have meant nothing at all. Taken together, they painted a picture I wasn't sure I liked. Sure, these could just all be songs Mom happened to like, which just all happened to be sad or angry but I didn't think that was the case. The playlist title suggested otherwise. It wasn't that I didn't understand the value of sad music when you were hurting. I totally got that. It's just that I didn't know mom was hurting.

"Forever is a relative term."
T.F. Forester

From Allison's journal dated November 12, 1991
Twenty something years before the accident

So I met a guy. At the tutoring center of all places. We've hung out a couple of times now and I really like him. I mean I REALLY like him. I feel, inexplicably like he's important to my future. Like maybe he is my future. Like he's THE ONE. And that's really stupid because I've never believed in that stuff. I mean really? There's only one person you were meant to be with forever and ever? That seems ridiculous. What if you never meet them? What if you grow and evolve and the person who is perfect for you when you're twenty is no longer a good fit for you when you're forty? But this guy, I don't know. There's just something about him. It's really early to say the word love and I'm certainly not going to say it to him any time soon. But it's flashing in neon in my brain. Kind of tough to ignore. Sarah once said she thought maybe I was too much of a free spirit to love one person forever. I don't know. I do fall in love pretty easily. But that doesn't mean I can't commit to a guy. I don't know. I'm just thinking about him all the time. I've had a bunch of boyfriends before but nobody that I wanted to talk to *all* the time. I've been in love before. This isn't my first rodeo, as they say. But I never felt this way about anybody before. We'll see what happens. Who knows? But the way I feel right now, I might never love anybody else again.

From Allison's "Things Fall Apart" Playlist
41)We Just Disagree-Dave Mason
42)You've Got To Hide Your Love Away-The Beatles
43)Can't Make You Love Me-Bonnie Raitt
44)Key Largo-Bertie Higgins
45)Sorry-Buckcherry
46)Apologize-One Republic
47)Haunted When the Minutes Drag-Love and Rockets
48)Bring On the Dancing Horses-Echo and the Bunnymen
49)Crazy Life-Toad the Wet Sprocket
50)Two Out Of Three Ain't Bad-Meatloaf
51)Sooner of Later-Alan Parsons Project
52)One-U2
53)One Headlight-The Wallflowers
54)Desolation Row-Bob Dylan
55)People Ain't No Good-Nick Cave and the Bad Seeds

"No one is gone
who lives on in our memory
Yet loss is still heartbreaking
And frustrating
Because your love has no place to land."
T.F. Forester

Adam
December
Five months after the accident

It was just supposed to be fun. No commitments. No strings. Love was never part of the plan. How stupid could I have been to let myself fall in love with her? She was only ever supposed to be in my bed, not in my heart. And there's no way she was supposed to infiltrate my soul. Yet here I am, five months after Allison's death and she is still very much here, even though she is also gone. It's maddening. My apology to David didn't go quite as planned. Shocker. It was supposed to absolve me of my guilt. Now I just feel bad for both of us. How stupid is that?

And it's worse than that. Allison has me wanting to be a better person somehow. My life was totally fine the way it was. There are people who might have said I was shallow or superficial. There are people who might have said I was just coasting along. What's wrong with coasting? It's easy. Shouldn't life be easy if it can? I'm thinking about things now. I'm really looking at myself and my life and it's difficult. I don't want to have a damn spiritual awakening. From what I've seen so far, it's prickly and unpleasant. I could just as happily go back to sleep and remain unenlightened. No thank you. Except I can't. As hard as I try to go backwards, it just isn't happening.

I was always good at photography. But I also had trust fund money. I had the luxury of going to school for something I liked to do anyway. I had the luxury of starting a business doing something I wanted to do. I took pictures professionally than branched into teaching workshops and seminars. It was fun. It was something to do. In my family, we're supposed to have vocations even though we have money. We're supposed to engage in business of some sort, so I did.

Creating the fellowship was a whim really. The scheduling of workshops was getting tiresome. I didn't *need* the money they generated. I thought maybe it would be fun to work with just one student for say, a year. Then I could feel like I was mentoring. It would have looked weird to give the fellowships away for free so I created a "scholarship" and encouraged everyone to "apply" for it.

Sure, I could have made even more money but I didn't care. The first two students had come from the workshops I'd taught. By the time I met Allison and encouraged her to apply for the fellowship, I had already decided that I was done. I wasn't going to do it anymore. But I met Allison and thought "what the hell? One more student. Might be fun. Especially *that* student."

Now Allison has got me thinking I need to actually *do* something with my life. The crazy thing is if she was still here, I don't know that I'd feel quite so inspired. Something about her loss propels me forward now. It's as if I have been sleepwalking through my entire life and I am only just now finally awake. Maybe it's time to stop coasting. Perhaps the path of least resistance is not my path. I can't tell you how much that irritates me. Goddamn it, Allison.

From Allison's Journal dated June 2014
One month before the accident

Obsession. It's not just a perfume. I've been passionate. I've been focused but the descent into obsession is new for me. I don't like it. I don't like the woman I'm becoming but I feel powerless to stop. I think about two things. Drinking and Adam. Oh, I think of the girls and even Dave. I try hard to stay present but my mind always end up drifting back to alcohol and Adam.

The two have gotten connected somehow in my head. It doesn't even make any sense. I know that Adam is getting frustrated with my drinking. I don't know if he's worried about me or simply bored with me. I felt like drinking made me fun but maybe I'm wrong. Maybe I'm the only person who thinks that.

I care about Adam. I might even love him. I don't *not* love David though. As lost as I am, we still have moments where we really connect. We laugh. We touch. We relate in a way that only two people who have been together for two decades can. It's comfortable. It's safe. But it likely won't be enough to save me. Or him. Or maybe any of us.

Jenna came home from school and something is wrong. I've tried a little bit to get her to talk to me but she's not quite ready. In the past, I would have been able to draw it out of her immediately. In the past, I might have even known what was wrong just by looking at her. I've done it before. I knew that Steven Thomas broke her heart in the seventh grade. I knew when she got accepted at the college she wanted to go to. I knew these things without asking her. Without quizzing her. I just knew. Maybe I am too much in my own head these days to intuit things about anyone else. I need to fix that. I just don't know how.

April is sad and anxious but uses her anger to cover it up. I get it. I've been trying to hide sad and anxious for years. I hide behind perfection though, not anger. But hiding is hiding and I'm so sorry that April seemed to get this sadness and anxiety form me. Would that I could have given her something else.

Charlotte is both older and younger than she seems. She has a certain wisdom. She is an old soul. But she is also still really a baby. Wisdom without experience can be a dangerous thing.

My girls mean everything to me. They always have, but it's like a chasm has opened up between us. I can't reach them anymore somehow. I've finally realized that maybe the thing that has come between is is my drinking. My affair with Adam.

It's not just the girls and Dave either. My mother thinks I have a problem. I laughed it off but I wanted to cry. I wanted to hug her and tell her she was right. I wanted to ask for her help but I didn't know how.

Sarah is angry with me. She doesn't understand the affair. She's always thought Dave was the best thing that ever happened to me. I've known Sarah a long time and she's pretty much seen every guy I've ever been interested in or dated for since eighth grade, so she's probably right. I ambushed her with Adam. I wanted her to meet him so badly. I wanted her to understand who he was and who I was around him so she could understand why I needed him in my life. It wasn't fair of me, I know. She may not realize it but I've always wanted her approval. I do crazy things sometimes but I always want Sarah to say it's okay. Even if she's laughing at me and saying that's just Allison being Allison. I can't bear it when she doesn't approve or when I feel like I don't have her support.

Things have gotten so wrong with everybody in my life. I need to fix things. Maybe just maybe, I can do that if I can get a handle on my drinking. The fourth of July is coming up soon. That seems like as good a day as any to give it up. Sure, I could randomly stop on this Tuesday in June but I feel like I will have better success if I link it to a big day. I don't know why that is. Maybe I'm just being ridiculous. Maybe I'm just stalling for time. That seems more likely. I know I need to stop. I know it's important but I'm not sure I'm ready.

I need to be different somehow. I need to be a different person. I need to be a better person. I just don't know how.

"If I could manage to be alone forever, I would.
Needing people only leads to heartbreak."
T.F. Forester

April
December
Five months after the accident

I'm so mad about having to go back to sharing a room with Charlotte. I mean she's okay but sharing is a pain. I loved being able to have my own space. Interacting with people is just painful most of the time. They have expectations. You have expectations. Everybody ends up disappointed or annoyed. It's easier to just not interact with people at all sometimes.

I admit that Charlotte and I used to be pretty tight but I never know what goes on in her head. I suppose I could just ask her. That seem hard though. And weird. Besides, sometimes I'm not even sure what's going on in my own head. At least they didn't ask me to share with Jenna's baby. I suppose that's something.

I haven't seen Elise since our fight so I don't really have an outlet anymore. I have to be home all the time which sucks. I found a guy who would buy for me. He charges me a lot more than the alcohol costs but it could be worse. He could be charging me favors if you know what I mean.

So I got a job at the little coffee place down the street. Everyone was all like "Oh, great job, April. You're showing responsibility, blah, blah, blah." They can think whatever they want. Who cares? I'm getting what I want. Most of my paycheck goes to vodka but it's totally worth it.

I've found that flavored vodka works well. I can mix it with soda and you can't even tell it's in there. Or I can mix it with that stuff you use to flavor your water. I used some of my paycheck to buy one of those nice water bottles. Again, I got kudos. "Oh, look, April is drinking her water. Hydrating. Taking good care of herself." I *am* taking care of myself, just not in a way that most people would recognize. It serves me to allow people to think these things about me. It deflects from the reality and that suits me fine. The less people see me the better.

I've made friends with the school nurse. I'm in her office a lot complaining of migraines and stomach aches. She knows all about what happened with mom. She actually went to high school with her and I think she has a soft spot for mom and thus for me. You're supposed to have parental consent to be dismissed from school but the school nurse dismisses me often anyway. I try to balance it out. I don't go as often as I'd like and I don't go so often that she gets suspicious. But I go often enough to get myself out of at least part of the school day about once a week. The school nurse feels bad for me and I play that.

Dad works. Grandma talked Jenna into getting a part-time job too, so she wouldn't be sitting around all day being sad or whatever. Charlotte gets home later than I do. So nobody even knows if I leave school earlier than I should. I go home and I read. I love Hemingway and Edgar Allen Poe and John Green. Reading is almost as good an escape as drinking. Sometimes I do both at once. I drink to not feel things. I read to feel *other* people's things, which is always better than dealing with my own nonsense.

"The voice of your heart speaks softly
It can be hard to discern
Over the relentless chatter of your mind
But listen
And it will become louder
And easier to hear."
T.F. Forester

Charlotte
December
Five months after the accident

Intuition is a funny thing. Most people seem to think you either have it you don't. Or they discredit it completely and don't pay attention to it at all. I think some people are just more intuitive than others. But, I also think that it's like a muscle. If you listen, be still, and pay attention you can access that intuition and the more you do that, the better it becomes and the easier it gets.

I think Mom had very good intuition but I'm not sure that it's anything she ever gave herself credit for. Maybe she didn't even realize she had it. We never talked about it. Add that to the list of things I will never be able to do with my mom. The list grows longer all the time. I hate it, but I can't seem to stop adding to it. The prom. College. My wedding. My kids. I have to stop thinking like this. It's painful and unhelpful.

April and I are back to sharing a room. April is unhappy about it of course but I try not to take it personally. It isn't personal. It's just April being April. I secretly hope that the proximity will allow us to reconnect. I don't precisely know how to approach it but I'm thinking it over. We all need each other now that mom is gone. Mom had the ability to hold us all together as a family. I don't know what she did but we don't seem to be very good at whatever it was. And us all being separate people isn't going to help us heal our grief. I heard a quote once which said "In unity there is strength and since we must be strong, we must also be one." I don't know who said it but it totally makes sense to me.

I'm doing okay with everybody else but *nobody* seems to be making progress with April. Oh, they were proud of her for getting a job and all. But it still seems like they aren't really connecting with her. I'm not either. Not yet.

April hates school. Sometimes I find it frustrating too. But it's a means to an end for me. I like learning. If I put up with the drama that goes along with other kids and teachers, then I can learn. If I can learn, I do something that eventually I want to do. I don't know what that is yet but I will figure it out. I have time.

One day in early December, I'm sitting in English class, studying the Odyssey and I have the very strong sense that I need to go home. Right then. This is odd for me. I've never had this sort of feeling before. But I feel very strongly that I need to listen to it. Class is almost over. I ponder my options. I could go to the school nurse. But then she'll call dad or grandma to come get me. I'm not sure that's my best choice. I feel like I need to go home but something also tells me maybe I need to go alone. I could just sneak out. I never have done that but I don't think it would be hard.

When the bell rings, I hide in the girl's room at the far end of the hall. Nobody much uses that one because it's too far away. You can't get back to class in time. We only have a couple of minutes between classes. Nobody wants to be stuck having to hustle that much. If you have to use the bathroom, you're probably already pressed for time. Plus, the far bathroom is close to a stair case. I might get caught, true, but the same intuition which tells me I need to go home, also tells me that I'm not going to get caught. Not today.

It's like being on autopilot and it's bizarre. I am simultaneously very certain that I'm doing what I need to, yet totally unsure of the why. Don't ask why, a voice in my head insists. You don't need to know why right now. It will become clear later. Don't ask. Just do. I think of Star Wars. What is it Yoda said? Do or do not do. There is no try.

It's nothing to sneak out of school and walk home. It's not a long walk. I've walked home a bunch of times when I had an after school activity like chess club. It's one of the easiest things I've ever done.

Yet my heart is pounding when I pull out my key and open the front door. I'm not generally an anxious person but suddenly my anxiety spikes. I was fascinated last year when we read about the fight or flight response in science. I recognize that this is what I'm feeling now. I'm pretty sure there isn't a tiger in my kitchen, waiting to pounce on me but I peek around the doorway anyway.

In fact, there doesn't seem to be anyone home. As I'm thinking this and wondering what I should do with myself until everyone else gets home when I hear a dull thunk. It's as if something heavy has dropped to the floor. Weirdly, it seems to have come from my room. The one I now share again with April. My heart, which had slowed down a bit after ascertaining that there was no large cat in the kitchen, begins to race again.

The door to our room is shut. April has to be to school earlier than I do and she's been annoyed with me twice this week already for not shutting it when I leave. This pretty much sums up April and I. She is secretive and wants to be closed off. I am open and hiding nothing. I may not say every single thing I think, but if you ask me, I will tell you. So, I'm not in the habit of shutting the door. I'm reasonably sure that I didn't remember to do it again this morning either.

"April?" I call out, not touching the door at first. My voice sounds funny in my ears, like when you hear a recording of your voice. You recognize it but it seems off somehow.

"April?" I ask again. This time, I do push the door but there's something blocking it. It doesn't open in nearly as far as it should. I'm trying to wrap my brain around this. I peer into the small opening I've managed. All I can see is the edge of a black Chuck Taylor high top. I know these shoes. They were Mom's.

She always had a funky sense of style. There was a big fight over these particular sneakers just after mom died. Jenna thought she should get them. She and mom had the same size feet. April insisted that Jenna would never, ever wear black Chuck Taylor high tops and honestly, she was probably right. Jenna's sense of style ran more toward high heels or stylish boots. April had smaller feet than mom but she put them on anyway. And she refused to take them off for three weeks. She slept in them. When she showered, she actually hid them, who knows where.

Finally, Jenna relented and said April should just have them. April took them off to sleep now but still wore them most of the time. I feared she would wear them out but I understood the need to hold on to something of Mom's. Jenna had gone and retrieved her photos from the gallery. April had the Chuck Taylors. I had the journal. Even though I hadn't read anything in weeks, I knew it was there, tucked into a folder I'd had in the fifth grade, labeled "science notes" with a goofy looking skull and crossbones I'd drawn on it.

All this runs through my head both quickly and slowly.

"April?" I ask a third time. I'm beginning to get it now. My brain is starting to process what is happening. My sister is on the floor of the bedroom we share and she's not responding.

Suddenly, everything is all calm and reasonable. I know what I need to do. We were one of the few families who still had a landline. We all had cell phones. Dad was the only one who ever answered it. Jenna, April and I hadn't had anything to do with it in years. Yet, the landline is the one I pick up. My cell is in my backpack, which I've dropped in the front hall like I always do. Plus I have it in the back of my head that even though I can provide an address when I call 911, it will show up automatically if I use the landline. It may save a few seconds. I've never had to call 911 before.

We practiced it in school a couple of years ago but Mom had made us practice at home long before that. "You never know," she said. "It might be important someday and if it is, it will also be important not to panic. The way you get around panic is practice," she'd told us.

I hang up with the dispatcher. I try the door one more time but April is blocking it. I hate to leave her. I don't even know if she's breathing or what's wrong with her but it's going to take someone stronger than me to open that door. Even if I ran at it with all the force I could muster, that might jar April and maybe it wouldn't even be okay to move her. But I heard the thunk. How long ago was it? My sense of time, which is normally very good has gotten all fuzzy. I don't think it could have been more than five minutes ago though. My sister was upright five minutes ago.

I decide that going downstairs to wait for the ambulance is my best choice. As I open the front door, kicking my backpack out of the way as I go, I see blue lights. The police are already pulling up to the curb. That was fast. I lead the officer upstairs and he's just getting the door open when the EMTs arrive. I try to stand out of the way but where I can still see. Our room isn't very big. So I can sit on my bed which seems super awkward or stand anxiously in the hall which is only marginally less awkward.

I don't really know exactly what the EMTs are doing but I hear them mention her pulse, which has to be a good thing. At least she has one. The police officer comes out to talk to me. For a brief moment, I irrationally wonder if he's going to ask me why I happen to be home and not in school but I realize April is a more immediate concern. Instead, he asks me if she drank a lot. I'm confused. I start to tell him about her recent acquisition of a water bottle and how everybody was so proud of her for taking care of herself and hydrating. Then I realize that isn't what he's talking about at all. For a second, I think maybe he's talking about mom and her crash. Dad has told me only that mom might have had a few more drinks than she should have and make the bad choice of driving her car. He was vague about it but I'm not dumb. I know about drunk driving. I just never thought it could be something my mother did.

I shake my head a little bit as if I could get my thoughts straight this way. The cop isn't talking about mom. He's asking about April and it's important and it's not about water.

"I didn't know she was drinking," I stammer. Suddenly, I feel foolish and angry at myself. I've been trying to reconnect with April but I haven't really *seen* her despite believing that I did. The police officer is not unsympathetic. He takes my arm and gently points me toward the floor next to April. There is a big bottle which according to the label once contained vodka. It's empty. There are also several of those little mini alcohol bottles. What are they called? I can't remember. Blips? I know that isn't right but it's something like that.

"I can't tell you if your sister has been drinking regularly," the cop tells me, "But it looks like she's had an awful lot this afternoon."

One of the EMTs is older. The other one looks like he's about Jenna's age. The younger one doesn't say anything but the older one doesn't want me to ride in the ambulance.

"...not a good idea," I hear him say to the younger one, even though his back is turned. The younger one nods his head and says something I can't hear.

The older one says, "...can't just leave her though."

I want to say "I'm right here, you know. I'm not six. I understand what you're saying." But everything is so surreal. Time is moving strangely. I think those words but there is no legit anger behind them.

They have a very brief conversation with the cop and he comes to my rescue, saying I can ride to the hospital with him in the police cruiser. He verifies which hospital they're going to. There are two different hospitals near our town. It's the other one. Not the one one they brought Mom to. For some reason this makes me feel ridiculously relieved. As if maybe nothing bad could happen to April if she went to a different hospital. I know it's faulty thinking but I allow myself to feel relieved anyway.

The cop doesn't try to make conversation with me on the drive and I am grateful. I'm not sure I'm capable of conversation. I think about Mom and how she always seemed so calm, not matter what was happening. I wish I could be more like her in this moment. I don't feel calm. I've read some of her journal entries. I know she wasn't always as together as she seemed. But I don't want to know this about her in this moment. I want to retreat to the memory of her making Jenna and April and I practice calling 911. I want to remember her teaching us to be brave and strong because she always did. We never knew that maybe she wasn't always those things herself.

As we pull into the hospital lot, at the emergency entrance, there is a large digital clock which shows the time, down to the second in bright red numbers. If I had stayed at school, I would still have fifteen minutes left of social studies. I would still have a ten minute bus ride home after that last bell rang. That's twenty five minutes and that's if I didn't talk to anyone at my locker or linger to watch the lacrosse game or stop and buy a coke out of the machine or decide to walk home.

What if I hadn't listened to my intuition? What if I had decided that sneaking out was too risky or too complicated or that I was just being foolish? What if I'd totally ignored that voice that told me to go home? Because honestly, I think people hear those nudges all the time and willfully choose not to listen. What happens if April lies on the floor unconscious and surrounded by empty bottles for longer than she did? What happens to her then? I don't know. I don't even know what happens to her now. And I begin to cry. Huge, braying, "I can't even breathe" kind of sobs. I cry as the cop leads me into the hospital. I cry as they sit me in a family waiting room. I cry as I give the cop Dad's cell phone number and as he gently but urgently explains what's happened. Dad and Jenna and Grandma all get the the hospital around the same time about half an hour later. They are still working on April in the ER and I am still crying.

*"I confess I am making this all up as I go
and much of it
isn't even very good."*
T.F. Forester

Cindy
December
Five months after the accident

I question everything I've ever done as a mother and as a grandmother. The hospital family room is empty at 2 in the morning. I've sent David home with Charlotte who looked like she'd been through the ringer. He went very reluctantly and I don't blame him. How do you put the needs of one daughter ahead of another's? I promised to call him if anything changed. He will be back shortly anyway, I suspect. I made Jenna go home two hours before that. She didn't look much better than Charlotte did and she had the baby to think about.

I've come looking for some coffee. The cafeteria isn't open in the middle of the night but someone told me there is a Keurig in the family room. I'm not going home any time soon. I kept dozing off, sitting next to April's bed and I wanted to be awake if she woke up. I wanted to be there and fully alert if she needed me. Even now, it pains me to be away from her for these few minutes while I've come to seek out caffeine.

She drank an awful lot. They found Xanax and Percocet in her system too. God knows where she got them but it's not that hard to get these things anymore, I guess. Maybe it never was. They didn't pump her stomach. I guess that's not something they usually do with alcohol anymore. They had her intubated for a while though. She was going to be physically okay, they thought.

I miss Allison so much in this moment. Allison always appeared completely confident in her mothering skills. She should have been. She was a great mother. If she had doubts, she didn't share them with me. Part of me was incredibly proud of her sense of security. Part of me was a little jealous. I second guessed my decisions all the time, especially around mother hood. It was ironic that I had managed to raise a woman who seemed so much better at being a mother than her own mother. Yet Allison was drinking herself. Could she have helped her daughter?

You don't stop worrying when your kids become adults. You just worry in a different way. It's more frustrating in some ways. More paralyzing. You can't set up play dates. You might not know their friends. You can't physically remove them from a dangerous situation like you did when they were little.

Earlier tonight, April was actually conscious for a bit and in what I consider a moment of great insight, David asked her the question I've had in my head since I got the phone call this afternoon.

"April, were you *trying* to hurt yourself, honey?"

He asked it straightforwardly and calmly even though I'm sure he dreaded the answer. I know I did. I give him credit. I really do. I know we've butted heads a bit since Allison died. I do know that my issues with him may be more about me than about him. I also know that he is a good person. A good father. Was a good husband. I hate that past tense but I can do nothing about it.

April didn't say anything at first.. I'm not even certain she heard him. He didn't give up though. Terrified as I was of her answer, I might have given up here. He did not. Kudos to him then. I feel a pang that our relationship has been strained since we lost Allison. He's a good guy. I need to give him a break.

"April," he told her calmly, "We're going to help you. We love you. But we need to know *how* to help you."

April shakes her head slightly and it looks like even that small motion pains her.

David persisted. Gently, but he persisted nonetheless.

"No, you won't tell us or no, you didn't want to hurt yourself?" he asks.

"Didn't want to hurt myself," she says slowly. The words croak out of her throat like she hasn't used her voice in years. "Was trying *not* to hurt, actually," she admits.

The ramifications of this are not immediately clear. While it's a relief to know that suicide wasn't her goal, it's also clear that she's really struggling. I think we all are.

From Allison's Journal, Dated January 14, 2014
Six months before the accident

David and I went out to dinner tonight. It's been a long time since we've done that. We used to be great at regular date nights, even when the girls were little. Lately though it's like we've forgotten. He doesn't ask and neither do I. Part of me doesn't mind. My thoughts are often elsewhere and it takes a lot of energy for me to remain present sometimes. Yet I also know that my marriage is failing and that a good chunk of the responsibility for that failure lies with me. I should try to repair things. It would be easy or maybe not, but it's the right thing to do. Yet sometimes, I am so much in my own head, it just doesn't seem like I am even capable of making the effort. Like all of my energy is taken up by just existing.

But sometimes I rally. Sometimes I almost feel like my old self and I know that I need to reach for my husband across this ever widening abyss. So when David suggested that we should go to dinner tonight, I asked if it was a date. Really, he was just craving Chinese food. He was ambivalent about the whole date piece. I was temporarily annoyed. It was hard for me to make an effort yet I was making one and he didn't seem to care. Did he not know how close to the edge we were? Well, of course he didn't. It wasn't as if I'd been precisely forthcoming with that information.

I took a few deep breaths. It wasn't that he was opposed to the idea of a date with me. He just didn't seem excited either. Maybe that's not a thing. Maybe you can't get excited about a date with someone you've been married to for two decades. I wasn't excited either if we're being honest. But I swear to God, I was trying.

We sat at a ridiculously long table. I thought of all those movies where the rich couples share a meal at opposite ends of ridiculously long tables. I thought about moving my chair over but it felt too awkward. We chatted cordially and pleasantly but with no real interest or emotion. I used to want to hear everything about his day and he about mine.

Now it almost feels like we're thinking "are you done yet?" even though neither of us would ever say this to the other even on our worst days. We don't fight really. That might be better. At our worst we're just sort of checked out or irritated with one another.

I went to great lengths to keep my phone in my purse. I wanted to take it out in the worst way but I willed myself to stay present. Isn't it awful that the technology is so addictive that we use it to check out and numb ourselves especially in situations where's it's really important to be where we are. I see families in restaurants with every member on some sort of device.

I see parents at the playground or the grocery store tending to the kid with one hand and holding the phone with the other. And my observations and disgust make me no less susceptible to the seductive pull of that technology. David often even forgets he owns a phone. He seems almost oblivious to its lure. I find myself unreasonably irritated by this at this juncture.

Why? Who knows? Well, actually, I know. I'm irritated because irritated is easier than guilty. I'm irritated because if things fall apart for us and somehow I'm looking at the very real possibility that they might, then I can say "Oh, we were struggling. Things were far from perfect. We often irritated each other.

It wasn't really true though. I find myself frequently irritated in general but I'm pretty sure that's my issue. David seems distant and we feel disconnected in some way. Maybe those are my issues too. Maybe those are just my perceptions. Maybe that's just how I am seeing things at the moment.

"Write the words you cannot speak, my love
Put pen to paper
Fingers to keyboard
And pour out your heart
Your fears
Your pain
Your precious, sweet, unnameable love
Even your darkness
Write it all."
T.F. Forester

Jenna
January
Six months after the accident

I made a discovery. Dad cleaned out all of mom's stuff last month and I've been living in their old room for a few weeks now. I felt a little bad about booting Dad out of his room but he said it was no big deal. It was the biggest room after all, so it made sense for me to have it because I would need more space. Dad gave me this logical explanation, knowing the logic would appeal to me and I wouldn't really be able to argue.

Dad bought me a crib and grandma bought a changing table and found a rocking chair. I have no idea what happens when the baby is a little bigger. I'm not sure a five-year-old and I can comfortably share this space. But that's a long time away. One could hope, that eventually, I might actually have some sort of life and move out of my parent's old bedroom and hopefully even their house. I have no plan for any of that now. I'm physically very uncomfortable these days. Emotionally, I'm feeling kind of battered. Mom. April. I feel like our family has been through a lot. I can't think about the long-term future at the moment. The present and the very immediate future are about as far as I can reach right now.

Anyway, aside from the new baby related furniture additions, we kept the furniture all the same. Mom and Dad each had a nightstand on their side of the bed. I was trying to tie my shoes this morning, which I have to tell you, is not that easy when you can't see your feet. I've also been feeling weird crampy contractions for a few days now. Braxton Hicks contractions my OB called them. I try to do this awkward thing where I sit on the edge of the bed and rest one leg on the other. Then, I can kind of reach. Kind of.

There's still an awful lot of baby in the way and this morning, my foot slipped and crashed into the nightstand. It hurt and I'll have a nice bruise but no permanent damage, I don't think. In the process of kicking the nightstand however, I managed to jar the small bottom drawer loose.

I hadn't bothered to put anything in any of the drawers, although I did have a bunch of stuff stacked on top of it. Hair ties. A water bottle . A used copy of "What to Expect When You're Expecting". Consequently, I hadn't bothered to look in any of the drawers either.

I could see a splash of bright pink in the space where the bottom drawer had opened. I pulled the drawer out all the way. Three small journals lay in the drawer. The first was the bright pink that I'd seen. It said "Jenna" in elaborate curlicue stick on letters. The second was exactly the same size. It was purple. It said "April" in gold, straight up and down letters. The third was an aquamarine color and said "Charlotte" squiggly rainbow colored letters.

I went back and looked in the top two drawers. They were empty. Dad must have missed this one. I know that he put off dealing with cleaning out their room for a long time. He might have been rushing. Maybe he got distracted. I know he found his own discovery; cassette tapes or something that Mom had made for him in college. Usually Dad was pretty straightforward but maybe he had left them for me to find. It didn't *seem* like something he would do but it made me happy to think that maybe he had.

I started with the "Jenna" journal of course. The first page was dated March 14, 1995. My birthday.

It said:

Dear Jenna-

It's late and I am so tired but I am too tired to sleep. You are sleeping peacefully in your little clear plastic hospital bassinet. You are the most beautiful thing I've ever seen. You have a little tuft of blonde hair which sticks out from under your pink and blue striped knit hospital beenie. Your eyes are blue. Dad thinks they may change later for babies' eyes often do but I believe that they will remain as they are.

I can't tell you how much it means to me to become a mother. To become your *mother. Thank you for choosing me. My heart is so full of love for you, it feel like it might explode in the best possible way. I love my mother, your Dad and my friends and through loving them thought I had a real understanding of love. I was wrong. The love I feel for you is like nothing I have ever felt before. It is fierce. It is transformative. It is more than I thought I could ever feel about anything.*

I promise you that I will be strong and brave and anything I can to make you happy and to assure you of how much you are loved. I promise you that I will teach you how to be strong and brave as well. Perhaps we will learn some of these lessons together.

Someday you will read this. You might look at me and think I was so sappy and that will be okay with me. I just want you to know how much you mean to me. You are miraculous. And you are loved.

Love,
Mom

I read it over three or four times. By the time, I read it the last time, big, fat, soundless tears are falling. One plops onto the paper, smearing the almost twenty year old ink a little. I wipe it away quickly. I remind myself to breathe. I sit there for a long time. Finally, I skim forward in the Jenna journal. There are a series of similarly written letters, probably fifteen of them.

There aren't enough for every single year of my life but it's close. Some letters are a little longer. One or two are only a paragraph.

A brief check of the other journals, show similar letters. April has fewer of them than I do and Charlotte has fewer still. But they are there, in Mom's neat cursive handwriting. Can Charlotte even read cursive I wonder idly. They don't really teach it anymore. I smile to myself. If anyone can, it's probably Charlotte who suddenly seems way older than she actually is. She and I have reconnected in a way that I didn't even know that I was missing. Even April and I have been starting to talk a little since what happened last month.

I don't read my sisters' letters. It seems like an invasion of their privacy somehow. There was a time where I probably would have read them without any guilt whatsoever but I am different now. Besides, I am totally focused on my own letters. I both want to read all of my letters as once and to dole them out a little bit at a time.

First though, I need a tissue. Maybe several. Although I've stopped crying, my nose is running now. I get up to go to the bathroom to get a tissue. I'll have to remember to bring a box back with me. I haul myself up and put my hands behind my back. My back hurts all of the time now. It doesn't matter whether I sit, stand or lay down. Nothing really changes the discomfort there. I take a few steps like this; hands on back, leaning backwards a bit as if I could re-balance myself. Grandma calls it the "Pregnant lady shuffle".

I get halfway to the door and I feel something pop. My leg is wet. At first I think I've had an accident and peed myself. I have had to pee just about every hour on the hour in the last few weeks. I stop walking so I won't leave a trail to clean up. It doesn't stop. I think "that's so odd. Nobody pees for this length of time. Not even somebody with a six or seven pound baby sitting on their bladder." It's then that I realize that my water has broken.

"Can you forgive me?
Can I forgive myself?
Can we just bask in our awkward and
mutual absolution
And admit
We have no idea whatsoever
What we are about?"
T.F. Forester

Sarah
January
Six months after the accident

Is there anything that makes you more vulnerable than standing on someone's doorstep with a casserole? I'm sure there are probably lots of things, actually, but I'm still feeling pretty vulnerable anyway. I haven't talked to David since our disastrous encounter in October. Oh, I've wanted to. I just had no idea how. It's complicated. Isn't it always?

I don't know if he's still angry with me. I don't blame him, really if he is. We were friends. I shouldn't have valued Allison's secrets over his friendship. Of course, I know there was more too. I have always really liked him although I don't think he was ever aware of it. I certainly never told him although I honestly think Allison knew. We never talked about it but she was really intuitive. If she guessed, she never seemed to feel threatened by it.

It occurs to me that I lived a lot of my life vicariously through Allison from junior high right up until recently. I loved watching Allison vs the funky, flaming, flashing sign but never would have had the courage or even the insight to question it myself. All through high school, I did things because Allison was doing them. I liked things sometimes because she liked them. I sacrificed a little bit of myself because I thought she would like me better if I was more like her. I couldn't imagine being without her.

Allison being Allison, she probably would have liked me just as much if I had been highly independent and my own person. Maybe more. She never asked for sycophants and she was fully committed to the idea that people should live their lives as they wanted as long as they didn't hurt other people.

But fitting in matters so much when you're twelve or thirteen and everything seems awkward and awful. Our patterns become habitual. We come to accept them as a part of ourselves even if they are maladaptive. Even if they are no longer serving us. We get stuck and getting unstuck seems unappealing or downright impossible.

Even when I got married, it was in part because Allison had. In retrospect, I can admit that I wanted to be married way more than I wanted to be married to Gary. I had no idea how much work marriage is. I bought the fairy tale. I drank the Kool Aid. I believed the happily ever after would just happen. And it did seem to happen for Allison and David. If their marriage had troubles, for many years, nobody saw them. They made it look easy. It wasn't easy for me and my own marriage fell apart after five years. Truthfully, we were happy for maybe six months of that time and probably not all at once.

We had impossible expectations for one another. We talked about wedding DJs and dining rooms from IKEA and what to make for dinner but we never, ever discussed our expectations for one another or for marriage. If we had ever actually talked about them, we might have realized we could have never been all those things to one another. You think you're communicating yet sometimes words are just falling out of your mouth. It doesn't mean they make sense. It doesn't mean the other person actually hears or understands what you're trying to convey and that's if you can even manage to put your feelings into words in the first place.

What would the texture of our relationship have looked like if Allison had wanted to be more like me? I can't even imagine. And I still can't imagine why she would have wanted to be like me in the first place. In rejecting Adam, I was maybe finally becoming my own person for the first time in years. Allison didn't seem like that at all. So who knows, perhaps our friendship wouldn't have survived with me being more me. I should feel sad or betrayed by this, yet somehow I don't. I still think that every conversation, every interaction with Allison was a blessing.

I bumped into Cindy in the grocery store. She told me about April. She told me about Jenna's baby. I had always been pretty close with the girls even if David hated me now. So, I figured this was my chance to at least say hello. To maybe apologize. If I couldn't make things right, I could maybe at least make things okay. So I stand on the steps in the cold with macaroni and cheese in a Pyrex dish and I ring the bell.

David
January
Six months after the accident

When the doorbell rings, I assume it's some friend of Jenna's come to gush over the baby. They have been dribbling in, those that are still home on winter break and the ones who went to school locally. They don't want babies of their own, of course. In a way, they are secretly horrified. They don't understand how she could have been so careless. They don't understand what she saw in a guy like Jason. I never met the dude and I have no love for the fact that he broke my daughter's heart. But *she* loved him. That counts for something. I would never say "I told you so." At any rate, Jenna's friends are judgmental and I really dislike them for it. I can see it although I hope Jenna cannot.

They are clever enough to not show their judgment in any open way though. Openly, they coo at the baby, a girl who Jenna has named Madison Allison. I love that she used her mother's name as a middle name although I'm not sure how well it flows with Madison. But this is the least of my worries in my little world these days. Not my monkeys, not my circus, as April would say.

The visitors bring little, impractical outfits and large impractical stuffed toys. Jenna always tries to stay positive but I know she's not a Pollyanna Sunshine. She's a bright girl. Sorry, woman. It still dumbfounds me that soon all of my "girls" will be women. I'm not a 1950's dad. Sometimes I just forget the passage of time.

Anyway, if Jenna senses their judgment, she doesn't call them on it. She accepts their gifts graciously and lets them hold the baby, hastily taking her back if she spits up or poops or does anything less than adorable. I'm not sure if these visits buoy her spirits or she merely tolerates them but I know they will end soon. When the semester is over in May, there will be fewer of these visits and eventually, all but a handful will probably stop entirely. My heart breaks for Jenna but I also think she will be okay. She will find a playgroup. She will make some mom friends. Life will not be what she expected it to be, but then life never is. Not for any of us.

So, when I open the door and see Sarah, it is a welcome surprise. We haven't talked since October when things all went wrong. I know that I overreacted but I've had no idea how to fix things. Well, idiot, I think, you could have just called her and said "hey, I overreacted." But I haven't done that. I tell myself I'm still struggling with Allison's loss and I am. I tell myself that I've been super focused on keeping my little family afloat and this is also true. But neither of these is 100% the reason I haven't tried to fix things with Sarah.

What happened in October happened way too close to that guy Adam's confession. If I'd had some time to process his disclosure, maybe things might have been different when Sarah let hers slip. But I also know that if I hadn't gotten angry at Sarah for knowing about it, whatever happened next might have had a hint of revenge to it. Sarah deserves better and maybe so do I.

But standing on my doorstep in January, looking cold and uncertain, she is a sight for sore eyes. I hug her with enthusiasm although it's awkward because she's holding a glass dish of food. She tries to hug me back and ends up dumping most of the pasta on my shirt. She looks mortified and ready to run but I help her right the dish and scoop macaroni off my shirt and back into the dish. The futility of this gesture makes us both laugh.

It starts with a small snort chuckle and escalates. The more I laugh, the more she does, until both of us are laughing like crazy. We feed into each other. When one of us begins to subside, the other starts up again. We laugh together for a really long time. It feels so good. When was the last time I really laughed? I can't remember. But I feel like if we shared this, we just might be able to work everything else out too.

I don't know if there's more for us in the cards than friendship but this shared laughter is the best thing I've felt in a long time. It's a start. I invite her in.

"You say 'I can't'
Yet you would astonish yourself
If you just allowed yourself to
You have no idea, the things you are
capable of."
T.F. Forester

Allison's Letter to April
May, 2002

Dear April-

This summer was rough for us. But we got through it and we will get through other rough times. Last summer, when you and Jenna and I were catching lightening bugs in the park by our house, you saw kids playing baseball. Is it possible you never saw anyone play baseball before this? I don't think so. I just think it wasn't on your radar before that. Regardless, you were fascinated. You insisted we sit on the hard metal bleachers and watch, even though we didn't know any of the kids on the team and even though it got dark and we could barely see.

We went and watched again the next week and the next. All summer, we watched kids play baseball and you learned about the game. Then fall came and everybody went back to school and there was no more baseball and you were broken-hearted. But you are also strong and resilient (never forget it) and you drew pictures and learned to spell and all the other things that six year olds do. In fact, you adapted so well to life without baseball, I wasn't sure if it was just a passing thing or not. Sometimes we get really excited about things for a little while and sometimes we're really excited about things for a long time and both are okay.

Last month, we got a paper home from school, saying that teams were forming for the summer and that you could sign up. I asked you if you wanted to play baseball this year. You have to be six and you are six. (So even if you had wanted to play last year and we had known about it ahead of time, you were too young to play.) You didn't say anything for a while. I wondered what you were thinking. I know you won't always want to tell me what you're thinking and there's nothing wrong with that. But I want you to know, that if you want to tell me, I am always interested in knowing.

Anyway, it hadn't actually occurred to you that you could play the game. You knew you could watch, of course, we watched a lot of those games last summer. But you didn't realize you could actually PLAY. But you said yes. I was proud of you. It's great to watch things but it's also wonderful to DO things. And you were so excited. You and dad went and bought a glove. He's more of a football guy actually but he was excited because you were excited. We both were. Honestly, we don't care what you guys love and we support you with whatever want to do.

There were two practices at the beginning of the week and you went and came home happy. Then came a practice game. A scrimmage they called it. Dad and Jenna and I sat in the bleachers and watched. Halfway through, your coach called everyone together and said some things to you. I couldn't hear what they were. I hope they were encouraging. All I know is that when you went back out onto the field, your face had changed. Dad thought you were just squinting into the sun but I knew better. You were sad and worried. I just didn't know why. I still don't. I only know that when the game finished, you got into the car really quietly. You didn't laugh. You didn't smile and you didn't say anything about baseball. You said you weren't hungry for dinner and went to bed early. I came in later to talk to you but you pretended to be asleep. I understand. Sometimes we're not ready to talk about things.

I don't know who said what to you. I don't know if it was your coach or another kid. I just know that whatever it was made you feel bad somehow. Oh honey. Never let other people make you feel bad about yourself. If you love something you should always do it. Even if you don't think you're good at it. Even if other people don't think you're good at it. Even if someone criticizes the way you do it.

I hope that you will tell me what it was that made you so sad. We can figure it out together but don't let anyone ever dull your shine.
Love,
Mom

*"No one sees my hiding places but you
You see so clearly my distress
There is no point in hiding at all."*
T.F. Forester

April
January
Six months after the accident

So Jenna found all these letters that mom wrote us when we were little. Jenna read hers chronologically but I wanted to read mine randomly. After all, life is pretty random. If Charlotte hadn't randomly decided to skip her last few classes last month, I might be dead.

The first one I read was about baseball. I had totally forgotten that I once loved baseball. I had forgotten pretty much on purpose at first. But on purpose eventually becomes habit. Eventually it was like I had never thought of baseball at all and that was how I wanted it.

It wasn't the coach. He was really supportive. It was Jane O'Leary. She was seven and had played baseball before. She complained that I shouldn't be at second base because I wasn't really a fast runner. She didn't say it to me although I did earn a look full of elementary school contempt as she said it to the coach. He called her on it too. He reminded us that we were playing for fun and to learn the game. He reminded her that while she was a good player, she wasn't actually in charge. It was a small comment made by a small mean person and the coach had my back but it didn't matter. It broke my heart. It felt awful. I didn't want to feel like that ever again.

Looking back though, it might be one of the first times I truly felt anxious. I wasn't fast enough. I wasn't good enough. I wasn't enough. How could I play after that? I would disappoint my team. I would embarrass myself. Other kids would hate me and it would be my own fault.

On the first day of kindergarten, I fell at the bus stop and scraped my knee. It was a decent scrape which bled a lot. I spent the entire day, pulling my knee sock up over my wounded knee. Kindergarten was in the big school with the first and second graders (unlike preschool which had been only two classrooms).

I was terrified that my teacher would see my scrape and insist that I go to the nurse and that I wouldn't be able to find where her office was and I would wander around lost forever. When I got home though, I did something I seldom ever did. I lied to my mother. I told her I had scraped it on my way home. Because I figured she would have said "Why didn't you just go to the nurse?" and it would have seemed all logical and not scary when she said it.

Baseball was the same way. She would have asked why I cared what Jane O'leary thought anyway. She would have reassured me that I was fine. She would have offered to talk with the coach if I needed that support. She would have brainstormed ways that I could get faster or play a different position. There were any number of reassuring things she would have done to diffuse my BS. And yet even then, I was attached to my thinking. My therapist calls this faulty thinking.

I started counseling after what happened in December. It's not something I would have chosen for myself but the counselor is okay. Anyway, she says we all think things that we perceive as reality but aren't necessarily reality. She says we can change our thoughts. I'm struggling with that one a bit but I'm trying. Just like the scraped knee, Mom would have seen my baseball drama as faulty thinking right away, if I had let her. She wouldn't have judged or berated me. She would have helped me fix it. But I never told her.

I threw a tantrum. I said that I liked watching baseball but that playing baseball was not fun (it was fun until Jane O'Leary). Mom forcibly dragged me to a few more games, talking about honoring our commitments. She said I'd signed up and it wasn't fair to bail on my teammates. I didn't care. I was sure my teammates were better off without me and convinced I was a loser. Finally, when there were only a few games left, mom relented and didn't make me go anymore. She wanted to help me. She could have helped me. I wouldn't let her.

"Today is the only day you have
All of your yesterdays have been torn from
you
No tomorrows are guaranteed
Not for you nor anyone
You must navigate the now
There is nothing else."
T.F. Forester

From Allison's Journal
June 30, 2014 2pm
The day before the accident

The other day, I thought I'd use July 4 as a date to stop drinking. To finally tell the truth. To stop the affair with Adam and actually be a good wife for a change. And July 4 is only a few days away but today changes things. Today changes everything.

In college, there was a time where home pregnancy tests were incredibly complicated. You had to pee here, mix this, add that. Around the time that I got pregnant with Jenna, they introduced the one step type. Pee on the stick and that was it. Two lines meant positive. One meant negative. Easy peasy. Unless of course you got a result you weren't looking for. If you really wanted to be pregnant but weren't or you desperately hoped you weren't but were, then things got a little dicey. But you couldn't really blame the pregnancy test for that.

Now they're supposedly accurate up to five days before your period. I would have been thrilled to know five days early with any of the girls. Not that five days more of knowledge was going to make any difference in the long term, mind you.

It's amazing the emotions you can feel when you pee on that stick and wait for the lines to appear (or not). And I've found that they don't get easier to navigate than they were when you were seventeen and you desperately hoped you weren't or 22 and desperately hoped you were. No, that three minutes of waiting for the damn thing to process might just be even harder when you're 41. I used to track my periods religiously on the calendar. Go to a doctor's appointment and they always ask and I always knew. Then I stopped. It mattered when I was trying to get pregnant. It even sort of mattered from a "Boy, I better have feminine hygiene products on hand next week" perspective. But eventually, I just stopped caring. I was 41. I was in perimenopause according to my doctor, so I wouldn't be getting my period every month anyway. I didn't figure I was going to get pregnant and with three daughters in the house, there was always something available if my period showed up unexpectedly.

So when I realized I was late, I had to do some detective work. I had a period in May, I knew because Sarah and I had gone to the mall and she'd teased me about heading to the ladies room so much. That was before I made her meet Adam and she got angry with me. But June? June was a blur. I sifted through my mental calendar and came up empty. So no period in June then. That made me later than I would have liked but not very late. In times of stress, I'd been known to skip a month here and there entirely. I certainly had been stressed lately. And there was perimenopause too. I shouldn't have even been worried about pregnancy.

I held the stick with hands I was surprised to find were shaking. Sometimes I liked to pretend that certain things didn't really matter. My drinking. My affair. My complete feeling of being out of control. Usually, though, my body would intervene in some way and say "Nope. Not buying it, chickie bimbo. This is more important that you thought." Shaking hands were just one of the ways my body betrayed the truth my brain wanted to deny.

I took deep breaths while I waited for the timer on my cell phone to go off. I willed myself not to look. You could follow the urine's path as it flowed down the stick, making the line (or lines) change color. Don't look until the time is done. The instructions used to say that you can get a false result if you check too soon but the tests are probably so sophisticated now that it's a lot more instantaneous. Breathe. Wait. Repeat.

Two lines. Positive. Pregnant. I'm unreasonably calm, I think. Shock, part of my brain postulates. I am holding my breath without realizing it. When I let it go and begin to breathe normally again, then my mind starts to whirl. I'm going to have a baby. I will be 42. My youngest daughter will be 13 by the time this sibling enters the world. Father? My brain asks. I don't know. David and I aren't exactly burning up the sheets these days but we're not celibate either. I've been with Adam a lot but that doesn't mean it's his. This not knowing the father undoes me more than anything. I always had such contempt for those girls who got pregnant but didn't know by who. Now I was one of them.

I've just gotten out of the shower but I turn the water on hot and step in again. It's easier to cry in the shower. I hate the sound of my sobbing. It sounds pathetic. The water drowns it out. I still feel pathetic though even though I can't really hear myself cry. The more I think about it, the more I freak out. I sob until the water turns cold. Then I stand in the shower and sob a little more.

Finally, I pull it together. I think, "thank goodness we bought the house with two bathrooms." Nobody has knocked on the door or demanded to know what I'm up to or what's taking so long.

So this is my wake up call. Tonight I will tell Adam it's over. I care about him a lot. I maybe even love him. But he doesn't want a baby and he and I were probably never going to have a future together. That's what made it so exciting. I hope that David and I still have a future. I hope I haven't screwed all of it up. But I'll just be honest. I'll tell him everything and hopefully my honesty will count for something. I have three bottles of wine in the trunk of my car. Maybe I'll just have a glass out of one. It will calm my nerves and act as a lubricant for difficult conversations. Then I'll stop. Cold turkey. Can't drink while pregnant. Or maybe I'll just pour them all out. Yeah, that's a better idea. Pour them down the drain because let's be honest; I have a problem. Once I start, I can't stop. And I need to stop. I have to think about a baby now.

Tonight I stop lying to the people I love. Tonight I stop lying to myself. Scary. Both of those things are scary. Who am I if I'm not always together? If I'm not perfect, who is going to love me? I think of Jenna who pretends things are okay when they aren't. I think of April who worries all the time but covers it up with other emotions. I think of Charlotte who intuits things she doesn't fully understand or can't articulate. I am in all of my daughters. I do all of these things and more, although I don't talk about it. I don't show that stuff to anybody. Who would love me? But I am out of choices. I have no more options and maybe in the end, that is what will save me. I am far from perfect. I need to own that.

Maybe I have just one drink tonight. Just to relax. The conversation with Adam might be difficult. But tonight is the night that everything will change. I promise.

*"Your expectations of a return to normalcy
are foolhardy
There is no normal
There is only now
And it is different
From moment to moment."
T.F. Forester*

Adam
February
Seven months after the accident

Is there ever going to be a time when my life is not unsettled and upended by Allison? Like earthquake aftershocks, her presence keeps making itself known even if only in my memory. All is calm for a bit, then I am jolted once again. Maybe it lasts forever. Maybe this is what it really means to love someone, even if they're not around anymore, even if you're not sure if they loved you back.

I've decided to make the photography fellowship a real legitimate thing. It has a real scholarship now, not just an "I don't care if you pay or not" kind of scholarship. I hired real teachers and a real admin person. I rented space. It has a physical address. It's not just something I made up on a whim anymore.

There is only one problem. It's not money. I have more than enough to run this thing for a long time. It's not even a question of what do I do next although that is certainly a valid question which I don't know the answer to. No, the problem is that I want, no I need, to attach Allison's name to it. I want to create a legacy for her.

I'm not being all sexist or egotist here. I understand that she has already created her own legacy. She had children. She had friends and family who adored her and that is the kind of legacy not everyone can build. Mine is only something I can do with money and truly, I get that it's a lot less important and a lot less meaningful than the relationships she built. She doesn't need me to build or create anything for her. But I want to. This comes from my need, not hers. I have financial resources, so this is what I can do. One does what one can. And this is what I can do. Maybe.

I not only want to attach her name to it but I want it to be *about* her if that makes sense. Eventually, I understand that it will take on a life of its own, as it must. It will be about other people and their dreams and talents. But I want Allison to inspire others.

She didn't really start doing anything with photography until comparatively late in life. She had no formal training except for what I taught her, which honestly beyond a few technique things, wasn't all that much. Allison herself was a paradox of light and darkness and that translated into her photographs. She could somehow see that light and darkness and capture it in her lens. Her gift was in the way she saw the world and translated that into photos. I want people to know this about her.

Yet as talented as she was, there was always that self-doubt. That nagging, harsh inner critic which said "You're not good enough." She never told me this in words but I could see it in her hesitation. It went away when she was drinking but that was an ugly trade off. It was not worth it, but apparently there were times when she thought it was. I know that she was very careful about not showing that doubt to her daughters either. Perhaps she did them a disservice there. I know she wanted them to be confident and always believe in themselves but sometimes it's okay to not know what the hell you're doing. It's all right to be vulnerable. But what do I know? I don't have kids. I'm sure parenting like everything else, seems a lot more clear cut when you're not the one doing it.

I obviously can't use Allison's name without her family's permission. I called and left a vague message with David asking him to call me back. Unsurprisingly, he didn't. Then it occurred to me that maybe I could talk to the oldest daughter. She had come to pick up her mom's pictures and portfolio shortly after the accident. I gave her credit for having the presence of mind to do it. She wasn't hard to find. She had a Facebook page although frankly, she hadn't posted much of anything since right around the time her mom died. I messaged her. She actually messaged me right back and agreed to a meeting.

I find myself ever in a state of trying to redeem myself with someone from this family. This is my self-imposed penance, I realize. I couldn't redeem Allison. I couldn't save her from herself and I don't think she wanted me to.

Can we really ever save someone from themselves? If you are determined to sabotage yourself, you will. Although I do believe sometimes, we can toss a life preserver. Whether the drowning person grabs hold or not is up them. I don't think I tried hard enough to do this with Allison. I didn't see her. I saw myself. I might spend the rest of my life trying to fix that, if it even is fixable. But I'm going to meet with the daughter. Her name is Jenna.

"If we can put aside our differences
And just be kind to one another
What great adventures we might have."
T.F. Forester

Charlotte
February
Seven months after the accident

Jenna, April and I haven't been on adventure together in ages. And almost all of those adventures included Mom or Dad or both of them. I'm not sure we've ever been on an adventure alone together. I'm not sure that either of them sees this as an adventure but I do and it's exciting.

It's one of those weird February weeks where the temperature shoots up to almost fifty degrees. The snow starts to melt and you think spring might be just around the corner. You want to unpack your shorts and flip flops. Realistically, it's going to get cold again. We're probably going to get at least one more big snow storm. But it feels fabulous for those few warm days.

Originally, this meeting was supposed to just be Jenna. I'm not sure why the photography guy wanted to talk to her and not Dad. I was perplexed by this at first. I planned on subtly looking for clues to why that was at the meeting but then Jenna told us a secret. Anyway, to Jenna's credit she has invited both April and I to go with her.

"Look," she said, "I know we haven't always gotten along..." We all know she means April here. Even April knows it's a comment about her, but none of us says anything about it.

"...But we're sisters. We need to love and support one another," she continues.

I look at April at this point, to see if I can read her face. I wonder if she's thinking Jenna is being heavy-handed and dramatic but I don't see any annoyance there. That would have been the old April. New April is still fiercely in love with mom's too big Chuck Taylors but she's softer somehow. It's a cliché that you have a transformation after a brush with death but cliches are always that way for a reason. Sure it's been overdone but it's been overdone because it really actually happens.

"And besides, I need you guys to babysit," Jenna adds with uncharacteristic humor.

We all laugh. I have always loved babies, so Maddy was never going to be a problem for me. But April has become particularly attached to Maddy. She complained so bitterly when Jenna told us she was pregnant and again when we had to share a room because of the baby. But it bears repeating, that she is different now. I don't know that she's done working on herself but is any of us ever done with that process?

April
February
Seven months after the accident

Six months ago, this little excursion would have been my idea of hell. First of all, Jenna wanted us all to get dressed up. She said it was important. She said it wasn't a social visit, although she insisted that we would be social. But she said this was a business negotiation. That probably made it sound more serious than it really was, although what did I know? I wasn't sure what it really was. I'm not even sure Jenna knew precisely although she had tried to explain it to us. It had something to do with this photography teacher guy.

Jenna knew about him and Mom, which surprised me. She told us the guy had come to talk to dad back in the fall and said he'd been having an affair with mom. Jenna said she'd been in the other room and happened to overhear a lot their conversation. Dad hadn't said anything to us. I guess I get that. He either didn't want us to be disappointed in Mom or it hurt him to talk about it. Maybe both. As soon Jenna decided to meet with the guy, she told us what she knew.

"Look," she said, "I don't know why mom did what she did. We aren't ever going to know that. If we could ask her, then maybe we could afford to be angry about it, to hold a grudge. But we can't. We aren't ever going to be able to ask her about it and that means we may never be able to understand. I think we have enough to try to process without being mad at her for yet another thing we don't understand. Now, I'm angry that she was drinking and driving," Jenna added. "Really angry."

She was too. Jenna hardly ever showed that she was angry but you could see it in her face.

"That," she continued, "may take me longer to deal with. You can make your own choices," she added, "but I chose to forgive mom for whatever happened with this guy."

I marveled that she wasn't telling us what we should do, just what she had done. Right away, Charlotte said she though she would forgive mom too. I said I would think it over and I meant it. I wasn't ready to decide quite yet though. Maybe it was because I knew it was happening while it was happening. I felt that mom had abandoned us. By the time Jenna and Charlotte knew, it was like she had already abandoned us by dying.

I did mean it when I said I'd think about it though.

"You don't give any one a chance, April," my therapist told me. "You reject people before they can reject you."

So I'm trying not to have those knee jerk "I hate you and everyone else reactions". I am going to think about it. No promises. I did promise I would be nice to the guy today, at any rate.

Today is weird. Jenna always acted like she was in charge because she was the oldest. You'd think that being a mom now would make her super pushy. Instead, she has backed off some. She is more inclusive. She acts like she cares what we think. It feels like she wants to have a real relationship with us

Bringing Maddy was my idea and I think it's a good one. I said "Look, we don't really know this dude. I know Jenna said he seemed okay the couple of times she talked to him but what if he's not? How mean can he be to us if we have a baby with us?"

Jenna said I had I point but that I was going to be in charge of Maddy during the meeting. If she cried, it was on me to change her or feed her or fix whatever her problem was.

I was okay with this. I never, ever thought I would like a baby. But Maddy is really cute. Babies are like a blank slate. They don't have expectations of you other than getting their need met. Babies don't put conditions on their love. Sometimes I can get her to stop crying when even Jenna can't. I don't even mind poopy diapers.

Because Jenna wanted us to all get dressed up, I wore a skirt. I just wore it over leggings and with mom's high tops. Whatever. Jenna didn't even say anything about it.

"All those lessons
You hoped to teach me
The ones about bravery and courage and
strength
You would be glad to know
They did not go unlearned."
T.F. Forester

Adam
February
Seven months after the accident

My meeting with Jenna Montebello is scheduled for 10am. I peer out the gallery window at five 'til. I'm temporarily confused by what I see. Not one, but three well-dressed young women are headed toward the door with a baby in a stroller. The gallery doesn't open until the evening and the hours are clearly posted, so it doesn't seem like this is some random group of potential gallery patrons.

They're at the door before I can speculate further. One of them is Jenna Montebello, I can see, as they walk in. The other two are younger than she is. They're all very pretty but pretty is nothing that's so important. Pretty is easy. Together, as a group, these young women look formidable.

"Mr. Miller," Jenna begins a little stiffly. I don't know if her father told her about our conversation last fall. I have no idea if she knows what happened between Allison and I. Her tone suggests that maybe she does and I find myself oddly embarrassed and defensive. I try to pull it together.

I barely recognize the young woman who came to the gallery last fall to collect her mother's pictures. That woman was scattered and flustered. She was distracted. This woman was poised. She has her mother's blonde hair and walks like Allison too. Her eyes are blue where her mother's were brown but the similarity gives me pause. I have to drag myself back to the present. I forced air into my lungs.

Jenna continued, "I would like to introduce my sisters, April and Charlotte and my daughter, Madison." They stand in a little group and I sense...what? A solidarity. They are of the same mind. They are a team.

Oh my god, I am so not ready for these women.

"Your light dims
Your sadness is showing
Your carefully built defenses
Are crumbling
Your perfection
Undone."
T.F. Forester

From Allison's Journal
December 2013
Seven months before the accident

I am SO incredibly sad. I don't have the slightest idea why. Sadness makes sense under some circumstances but this sadness seems totally random. I can't fix it because I don't understand they why of it. It just is. Blocking out the sun as it were. Surely, I will turn to dust. Nobody has ever been this sad and survived. Sometimes, when I'm depressed, I can access the memory of a time when I was happy. I can almost feel a trace of a memory of how happiness felt even though I am miserable. Now, I can intellectually understand that I have been happy in the past but that is all. I have no sense of what that happiness felt like. It's like I have no understanding of how happiness even works.

I may have overestimated my heart. I always thought I had an infinite capacity for love. I thought that I could love everyone. I always thought that if I loved fiercely and with everything that I have, then I could save everyone from tragedy and loss and heartbreak. Now I think that the power of my love might not be enough to accomplish anything. You can't keep anyone safe. Not the people you love and not yourself either.

But I may just be able to keep the sadness to myself. Surely that keeps them all safe in some way, doesn't it? If they don't know about it, it can't touch them. Maybe it won't hurt them. This I can do. I can put on a brave face. I can smile and laugh and pretend everything is normal, whatever the hell normal is.

I worry sometimes that my sadness will leak out around the edges of my soul. That it will contaminate the people I love. But I have gotten very good at sealing that sadness in. If it proves toxic for me, than so be it, as long as it doesn't hurt anyone else.

From Allison's Photography Show- September 2013

*"We shared so much
But we didn't share everything
Does anyone ever really share everything?
I do not know
I know only that it is too late."*
T.F. Forester

Cindy
March
Eight months after the accident

The house is quiet. This house is never quiet. For a moment, I actually can't identify what it is that's off. The silence is almost a noise in itself.

I'm here to watch the baby and she is napping. Last month, Jenna met with Allison's photography teacher. Apparently, he was also her lover. I never met the guy although I guess Sarah, the girls and even David had. They told me he was at the black and white photography exhibit Allison did. I was there but I don't remember meeting him or talking to him.

I had no idea Allison was having an affair. It makes me so sad. Not so much because she cheated on David although that's sad in it's own way. But I am sad because Allison had a secret she didn't tell me. We were always close although the relationship wasn't always easy. But is any relationship really easy? Maybe not.

Still, I always thought Allison shared a lot of her life with me. I don't understand why she didn't share that. Did she think I'd be judgmental about it? Did she think I'd be angry or accusing or maybe even jealous? I don't know. I'm sure she had her reasons for not sharing. If she walked through the front door tomorrow and explained them to me, I'd probably understand her logic. I'd probably be right on board with her reasoning even if it meant I was out of the loop.

But I can't ask her. I won't ever get to ask her. I am upset that she chose not to share this part of her life with me as her mother. But the real upset is deeper than that. It involves me processing her loss. That's something I seem to be doing poorly. Everyone else is doing a better job or so it seems. Why is it that I cannot help but compare? This is a failing on my part, I realize. Comparing yourself to other is unhelpful and doesn't let you grow. I know it in the abstract. I just struggle with it in practice.

Regardless, Jenna met with the photographer. She took her sisters and made them feel important. Even April wasn't complaining. I was so proud of those girls. I would have given anything for Allison to have seen them in that moment. The photographer wanted to create a program in Allison's name. He was clever. He didn't ask David who might have just been angry. He didn't ask me either. I don't know that my reaction would have been positive either.

But those girls...those young women talked and negotiated and managed to get something lovely from their mother's loss. My pride in them is only outweighed by my sadness that their mother can't see them right now. Although, without tragedy, perhaps they never get the opportunity to step up and really shine. Someone said that our circumstances don't create us so much as reveal us to ourselves. Perhaps this is true for them too. Maybe it's even true for me.

I've been Allison's mom for so long, I'm not sure who to be without her. Sure, I have a handful of friends. I'm in a book club. I work part time. But even after she got married and had kids of her own, Allison was always my priority. She took care of the girls and David. I tried to take care of her.

It's important to care for the people you love but maybe sometimes you have to put your needs first. It seems selfish but maybe is really selfless. I don't know. They say you can't serve with an empty vessel.

I can't go backwards and change things. Where I'm at now would never have been my choice but I have to deal with it. Maybe that's always the way with carrying on. The things which push us forward are things we never would have chosen. If we get to chose, we stay in our comfort zones.

Maddy stirs in her sleep. I pause listening to the nursery monitor. Will she settle or begin to cry? She fusses a little. Sort of half cries. Then I actually hear her sigh and it's quiet again. Robert Frost said "In three words, I can sum up everything I've learned about life: it goes on." And so it does.

"You know what you know
Doubt less
Listen more."
T.F. Forester

Allison's letter to Charlotte
March 14, 2014
Four months before the accident

Dear Charlotte-
I just wanted you to know that I think you're amazing. You might say that I'm supposed to think that because I'm your mom but I promise you I would think it regardless.

I know it can't be easy being the youngest sometimes. Your sisters are amazing women in their own right but they both have very strong personalities. You are quieter. You spend a long time processing things. I know this about you and I think it's wonderful. I just hope you never feel that you are lost in the shuffle or standing in their shadows.

Jenna is like me in that she always tries to put a positive spin on things, no matter what is happening or how bad she feels. April is like me in that she sometimes worries about things she can't control. (And just so you know, we can't control most things. We can only control how we react to them. That advice can be hard to follow when you're prone to worry but I know that you aren't.). Anyway, I think you are like me because you sometimes just know things.

It can be scary sometimes to just know things. Sometimes you can feel a certain knowledge. It shows up in your heart or your body. You might be confused. You might wonder how you could actually know something with out someone telling you or really seeing it for yourself.

But I want you to know that your intuition is a wonderful thing. It's a gift. I think anyone can work to develop their intuition. Like going to the gym and working out, that muscle gets stronger, the more you use it. But I also think that some people like you and I maybe started out with a little bit more than most people have.

I want you to trust your intuition. Never ignore it. If you feel something strongly in your heart, you're probably right, even if the chatter in your brain tells you different. This summer, when you're home from school, I hope we get the chance to talk about it some more.

I love you very much.

Love,
Mom

"Your memories play tricks
Even when you think you've been the most
reliable witness ever
We see what we want to
And only those things at which we are at a
point
To be able to see
It's funny what we remember
Or misremember."
T.F. Forester

May
David
Ten months after the accident

"You know happy endings only actually happen in books and movies, right Dad?" April asked me.

For a minute, she sounded so much like the old, unhappy, drinking April, I was concerned. It must have showed on my face.

"Don't worry," she laughed. "I'm still better. It doesn't mean I can't retain my cynicism though," she said laughing again.

She was essentially laughing at me and I didn't care. It was more conversation and insight than I would have gotten out of her right after Allison died. Plus she was a lot less angry. I could deal with a little cynicism.

Allison's birthday was in May. We'd had a funeral when she died of course. It had been a somber affair. Not only were we all so sad, we were all also in shock. It was so sudden. I suppose death is always sudden. Even if your loved one is sick for a long time before they die, you're probably never actually ready to lose them forever.

Regardless, one spring day it occurred to me that we should celebrate Allison's birthday. Not in some weird, morbid way but as a celebration of her life. I know they often call funerals that, these days but her funeral was definitely not a celebration of her life. No, it was a collection of Allison's loved ones sitting in shock, wondering why she had abandoned us.

I'm not saying I'm over it now. I don't think "over it" is even a thing. I think you integrate. I think you adapt. Maybe you never don't hurt again. Maybe it hurts forever but you figure out a way to keep living your life too. You keep going. Day by day. From this breath to the next. Because really, what other options do you have?

Maybe this isn't the perfect time to celebrate Allison's life. But then again, maybe it is. Despite April's semi-teasing, I'm not really looking for a happy ending. I'm not looking for an ending at all. It's actually more like a beginning. The beginning of how to figure out the rest of our lives without her. Who do we become? How do we chose to live our lives from this point on?

We always have these choices, mind you. It's just that loss drags them to the forefront of our hearts. They seem more impactful then, but this ability to hit the reset button is always within us. Stay or go. Persevere or surrender. Love or let go. We make these choices unconsciously every single moment of every day. The trick perhaps is to remember that we are making them.

So, a party then. To celebrate Allison. Parts of me are still absolutely hurt by her betrayal. By her failure to communicate her pain to me. But I have loved her since I met her and I do not know how to not love her. That love overshadows everything else, even now that she's gone.

Sarah
May
Ten months after the accident

David wants me to help him plan a party to remember Allison. We're finally really getting to know one another, even though we've technically known each other for years. I am relieved to have resolved our issues. I enjoy his company for its own sake, of course, but we also both remind one another of Allison. This reminding is often non-verbal and unspoken. It is far less fraught with grief than it was. It has grown into something more comfortable. It has become something which is much closer to honoring her memory and that feels right. There isn't more than that right now and surprisingly, I'm okay with that. I'm trying to remain firmly anchored in the present. And I am pleased that he asked for my help.

Charlotte
May
Ten months after the accident

So Dad had this idea to remember Mom by celebrating her birthday with a party. April and Grandma were afraid that it might make everyone sad all over again but it didn't weirdly. Dad even invited Mom's photography teacher. It was a little awkward but not nearly as much as you would have thought. Dad told Jenna that in order to really move on, he needed to forgive Mom and in order to do that, he needed to forgive Adam Miller too. It makes sense I guess. All or nothing.

Mom once told us that we don't forgive to make other people feel better. She said forgiveness didn't mean that we hadn't been hurt or upset by whatever happened or that we didn't care. She said that we practice forgiveness because it's toxic to carry that kind of stuff around with us.

I remember Mom saying so many things to us, that now seem wise. Yet I also know that she didn't always feel like she was wise. She was amazing but I'm not sure she ever believed it. I still wish I could tell her.

I had the idea that each of us should write down the stuff we loved about Mom. I felt like it might be uncomfortable to some people to talk about it, but writing seemed pretty safe. I brought a pretty notebook and sat it on an extra chair over in the corner of our living room. I wrote "I loved Allison because" at the top of each page, to help people get started. I explained what the notebook was for at the beginning of the party. I got a few funny looks, but throughout the day, I watched people go over and write when they thought no one else was really looking.

I confess that I did it as much for myself as for anyone else. Losing her, reading her journal, discovering that she had secrets and getting closer to my sisters, taught me a few things. You only know people through your own perceptions. Who you are as a person, colors how you see someone else as a person. And no one

probably ever knows *all* of you. People are never all one thing.
No one is all good or all bad. People are complicated. Even the
people who love you, perhaps *especially* the people who love you,
never see one hundred percent of what goes on in your heart.

So it was really important to me to know what other people
thought. It would help me see the bigger picture, I thought. I was
pretty sure I was going to need that, to go through the whole rest
of my life without my mom. It would help me cope and give me
some perspective.

Lots of people wrote lots of nice things. Obviously people
from her job or the PTA wrote more generic things than family
and close friends. They didn't know her as well as we did. But
maybe even we didn't know her as well as we thought we did.

*"Piece together your memories
Your different perceptions
Your favorite, fond moments
And make a quilt to keep you warm
In the chill of your loss."*
T.F. Forester

Charlotte
May
Almost a yer after the accident

Adam Miller wrote "I loved Allison because she loved life. She had no idea how amazing she was and neither did I."

Sarah wrote, "I loved Allison because she really cared about things, but more importantly, she really cared about people. She always made people feel loved and listened to. She always made people feel special, including me."

Grandma wrote, "I loved Allison because she was such an amazing mother. She was absolutely devoted to her girls."

Jenna wrote, "I loved Allison because she always knew what to do. She gave good advice and more importantly, she could ALWAYS make us feel better. No matter how sad or upset or angry we were, Mom always made it better. She couldn't always fix everything. In fact, she always encouraged us to self-advocate, stand up for ourselves and fix things ourselves. But just talking to her, always made me feel better. More secure. More grounded and like I could handle anything at all."

April wrote, "I loved Allison because she always saw me. Even when I was hiding or scared or angry, she seemed to know how I felt. She never made me feel foolish or like I was doing something wrong. She always made me feel like I was okay, just as I was."

I loved all of the responses, even the generic ones. But Dad's was my favorite. I re-read it over and over. It made my heart happy and also sad all at once.

Dad wrote, "I loved Allison because she was quirky and passionate and sexy and funny as hell. I loved her because she was devoted and smart and she was a bright spark in a dark night. I loved her because she was unsure and anxious and brave and fun and frustrating. I loved her because she loved kids and music and art. I loved her because she was talented but never believed that she was. All of this is truth and yet none of this captures the whole truth. There aren't enough words or there aren't any right words or words just don't work at all. I want to scratch out everything I've just written and totally start over but I think Charlotte would be mad at the mess in her project, which is a really nice idea by the way."

He left a big, blank space after that, then wrote, "I loved Allison because she was Allison."

I love this so much. And him for writing it. Because there are things about people which make our hearts want to burst with joy. There are things about people which make us want to tear our hair out. But when we love someone, really love them, it's a package deal. You don't just love them because of the things you like about them. You love them for all of them. Good and bad. Light and dark. In the end, you love people just because you love them.

The End

Much gratitude to everyone who helped with edits, read pieces and offered encouragement or listened to me ramble on about the story. You were all patient and wonderfully helpful.

Thank you to Linda, who asked, "Weren't you looking to get a picture of a rowboat?"

Thank you to everyone who offered up suggestions on Facebook for Allison's last playlist. I couldn't use all of them but I loved seeing such a passion for music and a diversity of musical tastes.

Much appreciation to the poet T.F. Forester who sometimes prefers to write under a pseudonym and who agreed to write fabulous bits of poetry as introductions to my chapters so long as I preserved their anonymity.

And enormous love and light for you, dear reader.

About the Author

Christine Beauchaine is a novelist, poet and blogger. She is passionate about art and reading and rescue pets and all sorts of music. She works as a toddler teacher at a childcare center. She is a certified
She lives in Massachusetts with her family. "Allison Forever" is her third published novel.

Made in the USA
Columbia, SC
20 May 2018